FIRST KISS

Hilary paused for a moment, still thinking, then added mischievously, "I made myself sound so virtuous, didn't I? To be honest, I will enjoy the evening—and who knows? I may find more material there."

"I am glad to hear it," Lord Grayden responded. "I wish for you to have as wide a range of choices as possible for your sketches. That may mean that you have less time to expose my foibles to the world."

Hilary looked at him directly for a moment, then said simply, "Thank you, Lord Grayden."

His eyes did not move from hers, and she once again felt herself slipping into a closer contact than she had ever known with anyone.

The time drew out, until finally Grayden said in a low voice, "You are a dangerous woman, Lady Hilary."

Before she realized what was happening, they had leaned so close together that they were only inches apart. This time there was no Miss Morrison to break the spell, and she felt as though she were entering uncharted waters. When she once more glimpsed the tenderness in his eyes, she did what she had longed to do before, putting her hand to his cheek and stroking it. Grayden gently took her hand in his, lightly running his finger over the palm of her hand and the inside of her wrist, then kissing the palm and pressing it back to his cheek . . .

Books by Mona Gedney

A LADY OF FORTUNE

THE EASTER CHARADE

A VALENTINE'S DAY GAMBIT

A CHRISTMAS BETROTHAL

A SCANDALOUS CHARADE

A DANGEROUS AFFAIR

A LADY OF QUALITY

A DANGEROUS ARRANGEMENT

MERRY'S CHRISTMAS

LADY DIANA'S DARING DEED

LADY HILARY'S HALLOWEEN

Published by Zebra Books

LADY HILARY'S HALLOWEEN

Mona Gedney

ZEBRA BOOKS
KENSINGTON PUBLISHING CORP.
http://www.zebrabooks.com

ZEBRA BOOKS are published by

Kensington Publishing Corp.
850 Third Avenue
New York, NY 10022

All Kensington titles, imprints and distributed lines are
available at special quantity discounts for bulk purchases
for sales promotion, premiums, fund-raising, educational or
institutional use.

Special book excerpts or customized printings can also be created to fit specific needs. For details, write or phone the office
of the Kensington Special Sales Manager: Kensington Publishing Corp., 850 Third Avenue, New York, NY 10022. Attn.
Special Sales Department. Phone: 1-800-221-2647.

First Printing: September 2001
10 9 8 7 6 5 4 3 2 1

Printed in the United States of America

One

Clara Dunsmore entered the drawing room as unobtrusively as she did everything else, slipping up behind Lady Hilary with no warning. Even the little terrier at the young woman's feet did not raise his head as Miss Dunsmore crept closer.

"I am going to miss you so, my dear Hilary," she whispered, her voice vibrating with emotion as she patted the shoulder of the young woman who had been reading in the deserted room. "I should call you Lady Hilary now, of course," she added contritely. "I must remember to do so. I just wanted to speak with you before you are called to your father."

"But why are you going to miss me, Clara?" she asked, frowning.

Hilary had grown accustomed to the self-effacing habits of her former governess and was not surprised by Miss Dunsmore's method of approach, only by her words. Lady Hilary Jamison and Miss Dunsmore had long been on a first-name basis, each being the only friend the other could claim in a household that ignored them both. "Am I going somewhere?"

Miss Dunsmore's lips trembled, but she made a brave effort to smile. "You are going to be married, my dear," she said. "I heard it from Lucy. Not that I normally listen to servants' gossip, of course," she added hastily, "but Lucy had just had the news straight from Fulton." She stopped, as though it were necessary to say no more.

Hilary closed her book with a snap. Fulton was her father's valet, and he knew her father's business better than Lord Werrington knew it himself. If Fulton said she was going to be married, it was undoubtedly so.

"It must be Mr. Brawley," Hilary said slowly, dreading even to say his name.

Miss Dunsmore's head bobbed in sympathetic agreement. "I'm afraid so, my dear girl." She paused a moment, then hurried into speech again. "Although I'm certain that there are some very agreeable things about the gentleman that you simply are not aware of yet, my dear." She peered at Hilary hopefully.

Hilary looked at her for a moment, then shook her head. "It's good of you to try, Clara, but there's no use pretending to myself. Mr. Brawley is—well, he simply is not a gentleman," she finished lamely, unable to say precisely what Mr. Brawley *was*.

"Even though his background is common, Hilary, there could be a great deal of good in him, I am sure," ventured Miss Dunsmore tentatively.

"You know very well that I do not mind that he has no title, nor that his father made his money in trade, Clara. A person may still have elegance of mind, even without the claim of family name."

Hilary stood and strode toward the window, staring out across the sunny September lawn. "It is not just his position in life, Clara," she said grimly. "Everything about Mr. Brawley is common—his mind, his manners, his conversation. You know very well that Papa is selling me off to him so that he and my stepmother and their sons will have a comfortable fortune to live upon, while I pay the price."

"Oh, my dear," responded Clara, her words catching

in her throat. "Since it must be, do the best you can with it. You know there is little choice for a woman with no dowry and no money of her own. When Lord Werrington sends Harry off to school, I shall have to find a new place—and it would be a comfort to me if I knew you were taken care of before I must leave. You know that you have never been happy here."

Ten-year-old Harry was the youngest of the five sons that Hilary's stepmother had borne Lord Werrington.

Hilary turned and flung her arms around Clara's thin shoulders. "Forgive me, Clara. What a beast I am to think only of myself when I will be leaving you alone here!"

The two of them embraced for a moment, feeling that there was some safety as long as they were together. They both knew that Miss Dunsmore's days at Werrington Manor were numbered; and unhappy though she had been with her students there—apart from Hilary—she had at least been able, as she always observed cheerfully, to earn her bread and butter. Once Lord Werrington let her go, her prospects would be grim. Finding a post at her age would be difficult indeed.

"Come now! What's all this?" demanded Lord Werrington, blustering into the room without warning. "Tears? And on such a happy day?" He spoke with the sort of false joviality that Hilary disliked intensely. Her father seldom spoke to her at all and never in a jovial tone.

"Come now!" he repeated, stopping beside them. "Set a good example, Miss Dunsmore! Show the girl how a lady conducts herself, particularly a young lady who is about to be married!"

He looked at Hilary as though he genuinely expected a rapture of delight. His daughter reflected—not for the first time—that this man surely could not be her father. Perhaps her mother had played him false and somewhere else lived her real father who loved her.

Hilary sighed. That was just a pipe dream, of course. This was reality and must be faced. She dropped Lord Werrington a brief curtsy.

"Married, Father?" she said innocently. "Am I indeed about to be married? To whom?"

Pleased with her reaction, belated though it was, Lord Werrington drew himself up to his full height so he could look his daughter in the eye.

"To Mr. Brawley, of course, my girl," he announced. "You could see in London that he could scarcely keep away from you."

Hilary restrained a shudder. "I believe that he did say that he found me 'interesting,' " she responded. That had been very faint praise, she reflected, but it was still far more flattering than anything she could think of to say about him.

"Interesting!" snorted her father. "I should say he finds you interesting! After all, you *are* the daughter of an earl!" He made this announcement as though proclaiming her the next queen of England.

"Of course, Father," she murmured, dropping another curtsy to placate him. It was true. Mr. Brawley would be delighted to marry the daughter of an earl, even an impoverished earl. Her father did not have two pence to rub together, and he was a profligate spender with a young family, while, according to the gossips, Mr. Brawley was as rich as Croesus. Mr. Brawley and Lord Werrington would be equally delighted with such a match. They should marry each other, she thought with dry amusement. Each would appreciate the assets of the other more than she ever could.

"When is the wedding to be, Father?" Hilary asked, dreading to hear his reply.

"No date has been set, my girl," he said airily. "You

are to go to Drake Hall to visit with Mr. Brawley's family. Once we have tended to the details"—and by that she knew he meant the financial arrangements—"I will set the date and send the announcement off to the papers."

Hilary frowned. "Do you mean, Father, that I am going to Drake Hall to be inspected? To see if I will do as a wife?"

Lord Werrington glared at her. "Are you mad, girl?" he demanded. "Some trumpery cit inspect *my* child to see if she is good enough to wed?"

Miss Dunsmore's hands fluttered imploringly at Hilary, and she forced herself to curtsy again to her father and apologize.

"Forgive me, sir, but I could not help wondering just why I am going to Drake Hall before the announcement is made."

"To give you two an opportunity to become accustomed to each other, and to let you see what your new home will be like. We should not wish people to think that we were rushing into this marriage without consideration. Mr. Brawley will be putting his best foot forward, as will the rest of his family."

"Ah yes, his mother and his sisters," murmured Hilary, conjuring up a picture of the terrible threesome with no difficulty whatsoever. They had no best foot to put forward. Harpies. That's what they were—there was no point in telling herself otherwise. She had met them in London and had instantly been repelled.

"And when you are at Drake Hall, my girl," her father continued, as though she had said nothing at all, "you must remember who you are."

She looked at him questioningly. "Remember who I am, sir?" she inquired tentatively, not taking his meaning immediately.

"You must remember that you are Lady Hilary Jamison, the only daughter of the Earl of Werrington. You must conduct yourself with an air of authority from the first time you set foot through that door. Everyone must know that you mean to be in charge after you are married. You will defer to no one save your husband."

Hilary stared at him. It did not seem to occur to him that she had never in her life had an opportunity to assume an air of authority, and that it seemed a rather late date to try to acquire one. A household dominated by an overbearing father, a domineering stepmother, and five noisy little brothers had scarcely given her the opportunity even to speak and be listened to by anyone save Clara. Indeed, the only point upon which she had ever asserted herself was the welfare of her dog, Jack. About that, she was firm. Where she went, Jack went. Since no one else cared for the animal, that had been accepted without any problem.

"I shall try, Father," she said finally, attempting to drive the image of Mrs. Brawley and her pair of daughters from her mind.

"Try?" he thundered. "You'll do more than try or you're no daughter of mine! Just remember who you are and hold your head high!"

"Why should Hilary hold her head high?" inquired Lady Werrington, who had just entered the room. "I mean, she should, of course. I've told her so myself dozens of times. It doesn't matter that she's as tall as a Maypole, she should still hold herself erect."

Lady Werrington, who was diminutive in size, never failed to point out to Hilary that she was far too tall ever to be accepted as a beauty by the *ton*. Since Hilary had no such aspirations, she had never been unduly troubled by her stepmother's observation.

"I didn't mean to stand up straight, Stephanie!" snapped her lord and master. "Try not to be so literal-minded! I'm telling her that when she goes to Drake

Hall, she must remember that she is my daughter and act accordingly!"

"Oh, that," responded Lady Werrington, dismissing the coming marriage with a wave of her hand. "To be sure she should remember. After all, she has you to thank for arranging such an alliance."

Because that was precisely what Hilary was thinking, but with a very different emotion from gratitude, she almost smiled at the irony. She had always taken her amusement where she could find it.

No one could ever accuse Lady Werrington of being either perceptive or kind or—as her husband had so sharply pointed out—anything other than highly literal in her understanding. And Hilary was aware, of course, that her stepmother would greet this marriage with joy. She would no longer have an unwanted daughter underfoot; instead she would have more money than she had had since marrying Lord Werrington. Things were working out quite nicely for her.

"When am I to go to Drake Hall?" Hilary asked, bracing herself for the worst.

"Well, there's no good in putting it off," replied her father, confirming her fears. "Mr. Brawley and I settled upon Thursday as the day of your arrival."

Hilary stared at him. "This Thursday? But, Father, that's only two days from now."

"Just what I said," he agreed. "It seemed wise to me to set the wheels in motion."

"Yes, indeed," agreed Lady Werrington. "It's not as though you have to decide which things to take with you, Hilary. You'll have the same wardrobe that you took with you to London. I will have Seton pack your trunk."

"You're very kind, ma'am," replied Hilary automatically.

"Yes, well, I am glad that you're going to get the

good from those clothes. They cost the earth, you know."

Hilary thought of the gowns that Miss Kilmer, the local dressmaker, had made up for her. They were well enough in their way, although Lady Werrington had chosen the colors, and they were anything but becoming for Hilary. She had one gown the color of mustard that made her skin turn almost the same color. She shuddered every time she put it on.

As for costing the earth, she knew that they had been modest in price. Quite different, in fact, from the gowns that Lady Werrington had ordered made for herself in London.

"And heaven knows they didn't do you any good your first Season," Lady Werrington continued relentlessly. "I really felt that we had wasted our money when you received not a single offer."

Hilary encountered Miss Dunsmore's sympathetic eye across the room and smiled as Lady Werrington began her favorite refrain. They had listened to her stepmother bemoan the waste of money the rest of the year after her first disastrous Season. It had finally gotten to be a game. Lady Werrington had two or three verses to her song of complaint, but she always returned to the refrain: Hilary had wasted their money.

"I must say I thought that you weren't going to take at all, Hilary." Lady Werrington let nothing stop her, once she was in full cry. "It was such a pleasant surprise, just on the eve of our return home after a second fruitless Season, to have Mr. Brawley call upon your father."

Since Hilary had scarcely looked upon Mr. Brawley's call as a pleasing event, she did not respond. After waiting for a moment, she turned to Lord Werrington.

"How long am I to stay at Drake Hall, Father?" she asked, wishing to know the worst at once.

Lord Werrington looked a little startled. "How long?" he asked blankly. "Well, what's that got to say to anything? You'll soon be married and live there all the time, so what's a month or so at this point?"

"A month?" repeated Hilary a little weakly. What he said was true enough, of course; and home had never been a haven for her, but at least it was a known evil. Drake Hall was quite another matter. She picked Jack up and hugged him. He had been sitting quietly beside her, listening intently to the tone of her voice and inching closer as he detected her distress until finally he was seated firmly on her foot.

"Well, that is one habit that you will have to give up," announced Lady Werrington, looking at Jack with distaste. "Certainly even the Brawleys will not want that animal to have the run of the house."

"Then I will not go!" said Hilary abruptly. "If Jack cannot go, I will stay here."

Lord Werrington, who knew they were on dangerous ground, silenced his wife with a glance. "Well, why should you not take Jack?" he asked, the false joviality returning. "After all, he will be with you when you move to Drake Hall."

"And thank goodness for that!" observed his wife tartly. "I believe I shall go and tell Seton to begin packing your things immediately."

"Just a moment, my dear," said her husband. "Which of the maids will you send to Drake Hall with Hilary?"

"Which of the maids?" demanded Lady Werrington, turning to stare at him. "I cannot spare any of the maids here!"

"You must," he informed her firmly, a most unusual measure for him, for he was an indulgent husband. "She is the daughter of an earl, and she will not go into Drake Hall without a maid of her own as though she were some commoner just come for a sennight."

Seeing that he would not be moved, his wife conceded unwillingly, "I suppose it must be Lucy. She is of the least use to me since she is not fully trained."

Hilary breathed a sigh of relief. At least Lucy, who was two years her junior, would not be intimidating. Lucy knew as little about being a lady's maid as Hilary knew about having one, and she was always cheerful when she came in to bring her a can of hot water for bathing.

She hugged Jack to her a little more closely. Thursday seemed ominously close.

Two

Hilary's heart sank as they drove through the gates of Drake Hall. The gatekeeper had emerged from his tiny cottage to open the ornate iron gates and swing them wide so her carriage could enter. Ahead of them stretched a broad carriage road leading to the imposing hall itself. She could see its massive outline clearly, uncluttered by any of the surrounding gardens and hedges she was accustomed to at home. And she was to be mistress of this cold and uninviting place. Closing her eyes, she leaned back against the cushions and clutched Jack and the hand of the maid Lucy, who sat wide-eyed beside her. How had she come to this?

The answer to that, of course, was simple. As she had told Clara, she was being bartered in return for her father's financial stability. And, as Clara had reminded her, her choices were slender. She could marry Mr. Raymond Brawley, as her father wished, or she could go home and dwindle into an old maid, which was precisely what they all feared was about to happen.

Lady Werrington had made no secret of her wish to have Hilary married and gone. If she stayed at home, she would simply be another mouth to feed, another body to clothe. And Hilary herself could see little advantage to staying, for she would continue to be ordered about by her stepmother and treated as a general dogsbody whenever something distasteful needed to be done.

No doubt when Clara was gone and Lady Werrington had grandchildren, Hilary would be expected to take care of them when they came to visit. Or worse yet, she would be shipped off to help with them at their own homes. Her only other option would be to become a governess like Clara, an option that her father's pride would never allow and that she truly did not wish for either.

Hilary sighed and closed her eyes for a moment. There was really no choice at all. She would become Mrs. Raymond Brawley and try to make the best of a bad business. Marriage must surely have some compensations.

For a moment her mind flew back to her first London Season and Lily, and she smiled in spite of her unhappiness. Lily Carlisle had been the beauty of the Season and an outrageous flirt. To Hilary's surprise, this entrancing young woman had befriended her and had kept her at her side during several of the first balls of the Season.

Lily had planned to marry as soon as possible, telling Hilary that once a woman was married, she might do as she pleased.

"You may even take a lover if you wish—after you provide your husband with an heir, of course," she had told Hilary, who had been shocked by her words, having lived a protected life in the country. "I shall have dozens of lovers," Lily had continued matter-of-factly.

And Hilary had had no doubt that she would do so. The outrageous Lily had married quickly and well, choosing a man older than she by some thirty years because, as she told Hilary, "He quite dotes upon me and will allow me to do as I please." Better still, her new husband, Lord Carhill, was a widower with grown children, so Lily was freed from the obligation of producing an heir.

Unfortunately, she had married very early in the Season, and Lord Carhill had borne her away to Italy and Greece on a wedding trip that had lasted for more than a year. That had probably been wise, Hilary had reflected, for Lily had a train of ardent admirers who would have remained in constant attendance on her had she remained in England.

Nonetheless, her marriage had robbed Hilary of her only friend and ally in London. Too tall and thin and fair in coloring to be considered stylish, she had struggled through the rest of the Season and returned ingloriously home, with Lady Werrington to trumpet her failure.

Hilary had heard from her friend a few times while she was abroad. The last letter had been sent from London just before her departure for Drake Hall. Lord and Lady Carhill had returned to England only a month earlier. Lily's letter had demanded that Hilary come to join them in London at once and spend a delightfully dissipated autumn with them. Hopeful, Hilary had asked her father if she could delay the trip to Drake Hall, but he had been emphatic in his refusal. She had not yet replied to Lily's letter, but promised herself that she would do so very soon. Just thinking of Lily put her in a more cheerful frame of mind. It was like having a door to the outside world.

As the carriage rolled to a stop, an imposing butler opened the front door and two footmen hurried forward to assist her. If Mr. Brawley hoped to impress her with this display, he did not succeed. Ostentation did not overwhelm her. Jack was equally unimpressed. One of the footmen attempted to take him from her arms, but a single imperative bark and a display of sharp white teeth discouraged further efforts.

To her dismay, instead of being shown to her chamber first, the butler led her to the drawing room and announced her presence to the three ladies of the Brawley household. Even though she had not been looking forward to seeing Mr. Brawley, Hilary suddenly felt that he would have been a breath of fresh air in comparison with the ladies.

Mrs. Brawley, flanked by her daughters Ophelia and Deidre, eyed her with hawklike coldness. In fact, their whole aspect was hawklike, all three of them displaying the same rather sharp-eyed regard of a predator for its prey. It was no wonder that she had thought of them as harpies. Hilary was horrified to feel laughter bubbling up at this irreverent thought, and she set her lips in a stiff smile, determined to stifle her amusement.

"I see that you have had a tiring journey," Mrs. Brawley observed.

Hilary was surprised by this unexpected display of concern, and she nodded, thinking that her hostess was about to suggest an opportunity to retire to her chamber to freshen up.

"Yes, it was a long journey, ma'am, and I am tired," she replied gratefully.

"I was not referring to the length of the journey, but to the fact that you have obviously had to contend with that animal you are carrying," returned Mrs. Brawley, eyeing Jack with marked disfavor. "Ophelia, ring for Rutgers and have him take the dog to the kennel."

Hilary stiffened. "No, Mrs. Brawley, Jack does not go to the kennel," she said sharply. "He is well behaved and he will stay with me in my chamber. I assure you that you will scarcely know that he is here."

Jack was the one point upon which she was determined to assert herself. His well-being depended on her, and for that reason she had brought him with her rather than leaving him at home, where Lady Werrington might very well have taken it into her head to give him away. She did not mind her husband's hunting dogs, which were to be found everywhere in the downstairs of their home, but she had taken instant exception to Jack when Hilary had received him as a puppy. She would, in fact, have ordered Hilary to give him up had not her husband overruled her. Jack had been the gift of Lady Connley, a wealthy neighbor who was fond of Hilary and felt some pity for her unhappy situation at home. Fearing the bad opinion of such a woman, Lord Werrington had allowed his daughter to keep the dog.

Mrs. Brawley stared at Hilary as though she had suddenly begun speaking Russian.

"Are you aware, Lady Hilary," she said majestically, "that this is my son's home and that you are an invited *guest?*"

"Indeed I am, ma'am," responded Hilary. "If Jack's presence is so distressing, I must apologize." Unaccustomed though she was to confrontation, she thought of Jack and straightened her shoulders, preparing to face the enemy. Her father had told her to assert herself, and she would do so on Jack's behalf.

Hilary directed her gaze to Ophelia. "Would you be so kind as to ring for the butler, Miss Brawley, and ask him to have my carriage wait for me? I shall be returning to Werrington Manor today."

Hilary was again confronted by the same hawkeyed gaze. All three of the Brawley ladies stared at her as though she were some unknown species that had just crawled unannounced into their drawing room, and they were uncertain of what to do with her.

"Return? Nonsense, you cannot return! Why, you have just arrived! What would my son say?" demanded Mrs. Brawley, regaining her composure.

"What would I say to what, Mother?" inquired Mr. Brawley, who had strolled into the room just in time to hear her last words. His rather slight figure was arrayed in fashionable doeskin breeches, a dark jacket, and tall riding boots. His dark hair was almost painfully arranged to achieve a casual, wind-tossed look. His manner indicated that he had no doubt that he was an impressive figure.

He took Lady Hilary's hand and bowed over it, frowning somewhat when she had to switch Jack to her other arm.

"Your very obedient servant, ma'am," he said in his best imitation of a gentleman's casual manner.

Hilary noted again, with some distaste, that he also had the family face. His dark eyes darted everywhere but lacked depth and expression, his chin and nose were sharp, his lips thin and colorless. She had almost managed to soften her memory of his appearance and his manner, but now she was confronted with the cold reality and her heart sank. This man was to be her husband.

Then, remembering Jack wriggling in the crook of her arm, she spoke, her voice firm. "It was very kind of you to invite me here, Mr. Brawley. I regret that my visit must be so brief."

"Brief?" he asked, startled. "What do you mean, ma'am?"

"Why, Raymond," began his mother petulantly, "the girl insists upon—"

"I insist upon keeping my dog with me instead of having him placed outside in the kennel," interrupted Hilary briskly, patting Jack as she spoke. "Jack is my pet and stays in my chamber at home. However, since that is not acceptable here and I have no wish to upset the routine of your household, I shall return at once to Werrington Manor. I have no desire to be a problem."

"A problem?" repeated Mr. Brawley. "You could

never be a problem, Lady Hilary. If you wish your dog to stay with you in your chamber, then stay he shall."

"But, Raymond, I really think—" began his mother again, but he cut her off immediately, throwing her a warning glance.

"Mother, we must make our guest feel at home," he reminded her smoothly. "After all, Lady Hilary," he continued meaningfully, turning his attention to her, "we wish you to feel that this is your home."

Such an observation was far from comforting, but she had at least won the battle, she told herself, forcing a thin smile. Jack stayed.

The next few days dragged by as though each one were a week in itself. It was difficult to decide which was more burdensome: receiving the attentions of Mr. Brawley or having to contend with the antagonism of the ladies of the house.

Hilary was well aware that Mr. Brawley felt no real interest in her. His attempts at compliments were so awkward as to be amusing, but she naturally could not laugh. Still, when he had caught her hand and pulled her toward him when they were alone in the library, the effect was not what he had hoped for because he had to look up into her eyes. Since then he had been careful to confine himself to close approaches only when she was seated and he could remain standing. She had never thought that her height could offer any advantages, but she was delighted to discover this one.

The Brawley ladies made no secret of the fact that they, like Lady Werrington, considered her height a marked handicap, and did not spare their comments. They had also taken to referring to Mr. Brawley as "poor Raymond," and the implication of the expression was unmistakable. Clearly, they considered her a poor bargain.

After a day or two, she no longer troubled herself with attempting any real conversation with the ladies, for doing so was a humiliating waste of time. They resented her presence and her title and found countless ways to display the smallness of their minds. Normally a cheerful person, she felt the atmosphere of Drake Hall settle upon her like a damp grey blanket, smothering her natural liveliness of mind and her ability to find pleasure in the small things of life. Drearily, she whiled away the days, wondering when the wedding would be set so that her misery would be complete.

Even the Brawley library, where she had hoped to find occasional sanctuary, was a travesty. None of the Brawleys were readers, and the books had been purchased only for show. The shelves were lined, although somewhat scantily, with handsome leather-bound volumes, almost all of which contained unread dusty sermons or antique scientific treatises. Mr. Brawley retired there to read his paper in state each morning so she had no hope of using it as a refuge, particularly after his first failed attempt at a romantic encounter.

Instead, she began taking brisk walks about the grounds with Jack—anything to free herself of the oppressive Brawley-ness of the house. She enjoyed the fresh air and the occasional conversation with one of the stablehands far more than anything that the household could offer. Too, it was very clear that all of them, including Mr. Brawley, disliked Jack. She was fearful of letting him out of her sight, certain that he would be mistreated if she did.

Although none of the Brawleys rode particularly well, the stable held several fine horses, and she occasionally took one out for a gallop to relieve her tension, leaving Jack with the stablehands, who made much of him. She often carried her sketchbook with her on their rambles, recording the things that she saw, everything from landscapes to grazing cows and small boys playing in a field. Also, being fascinated by people, Hilary sketched the individuals she had seen, concentrating on trying to capture their personalities in their expressions. Drawing had always been a satisfactory escape for her.

Finally, on a rainy morning a week after her arrival, Hilary sat down in her chamber and wrote a letter to Lily. At least the opportunity of describing to her friend what was happening and explaining why she could not come to London cheered her.

Laughter had always been her ally, and she and Clara had often made light of things that would otherwise have caused them pain—although Clara was often doubtful that she should encourage such lightness of mind in her pupil. Throwing caution to the winds as she wrote, Hilary deftly caricatured the Brawleys and related a few of their most outrageous bits of behavior.

They had made it abundantly clear that they wanted Hilary's title and the claim to her family, but they did not want her. Unfortunately, however, they had to take her, and they were doing so with very little grace. Hilary, who wanted no part in any of the charade, felt like a mere spectator in her own life, for she certainly had no say in it. Her only assertiveness thus far had been on Jack's behalf.

Having sent the letter, Hilary felt more cheerful than she had for days. Letters to Lily would at least be a link to the outside world. If she were going to be able to bear the rest of her life, she would have to find a way to make it livable.

At the moment it was better than usual, for Mr. Brawley had been called away on business and she had two days during which she would be relieved of the annoyance of his attentions. He did not really care for her, of course, but he alternated between attempting to pay her insincere compliments and telling her stories intended to impress her with his intelligence and his importance. The undertakings were equally unsuccessful.

Hilary devoted those two days to separating her mind into various compartments. She decided that she would think of unpleasant things—like the Brawleys—only when she must. She mentally sealed them into a small, escape-proof box. Instead of fretting over them, she spent her time searching for things she could enjoy about her life-to-be at Drake Hall. She was fond of the countryside, and she had her sketching and her riding. And she and Jack had found a few friends to chat with—none that the Brawleys would approve of, naturally—who helped her achieve some peace of mind. She was determined to make the most of the hand that life had dealt her.

Accordingly, at dinner on the evening of his return, she asked Mr. Brawley how often he visited London, hoping to hear that he went to Town several times a year. At least there she would be able to go to plays and visit the bookstores and perhaps even see Lily on occasion. Such opportunities might make her life as his wife more bearable.

"Oh, quite often, Lady Hilary," he assured her, smiling toothily. "And perhaps even more frequently now that I will be joining one of the clubs to which your father belongs. It will be much more agreeable putting up there than at one of the hotels."

Hilary's heart sank. It he were staying at a club, then she assuredly would not be going.

"What of your mother and sisters?" she asked faintly. "Do you not wish for them occasionally to accompany you?"

"My mother and sisters do not care greatly for life in Town," he observed pompously, ignoring the expressions of those ladies which indicated otherwise. "They prefer a quieter life, and now that your father plans to have us all to visit at Werrington Manor two or three times a year, I am certain that their longing for travel will be satisfied."

Hilary's heart dropped even farther. She knew that once her father had the marriage settlement in his bank account, he would extend no invitations. Lady Werrington would never allow the Brawleys to come as guests into her home. Undoubtedly Mr. Brawley thought that his sisters would find worthy husbands while they were houseguests there and—in his mind, at least—mingling with members of the *ton* on an intimate basis.

The conclusion was inevitable. Mr. Brawley would jaunt about as he pleased, leaving her at home to the none-too-tender mercies of his mother and sisters. They already disliked her heartily and once they realized that Werrington Manor would not be a part of their future, they would undoubtedly hold her responsible for their unhappiness.

When she retired to her room that evening, it was all she could do to face Lucy with any equanimity. Since their arrival, poor Lucy had cried every evening as she was helping Hilary prepare for bed. Her treatment at Drake Hall had been even worse than Hilary's, for the other servants were unmerciful to her, knowing that she was young and inexperienced. Just in case she fancied herself something special because she was lady's maid to the daughter of an earl, they had set her in her place immediately. Ophelia's abigail had been particularly cruel, always pointing out Lucy's lack of experience in a humiliatingly public manner.

That night Hilary forced herself to forget her own

Mona Gedley

problems for a moment and concentrate on what Lucy was telling her.

"Her name is Marie," Lucy said tearfully, wiping her eyes so that she could see to hang up Hilary's gown and fold her chemise neatly. "She isn't French. I think her name is Mary and she just changed it to make it sound fancy."

"Well, what did Marie do this time?" asked Hilary patiently. The last time, Marie had said at the servants' table during dinner that Lucy was too awkward to be a lady's maid.

"She said that she would press your gown for me— the gold one that you wore yesterday—for she said that I wouldn't get it right. And she's right, of course," added the girl honestly, wiping her eyes again. "And I thought that she was sorry for being so cruel to me, so I handed the gown to her."

"And what was the problem?" inquired Hilary. "Did she refuse to help you?"

"Oh no, my lady. She took the gown all right, but only see what she did!"

Here a fresh shower of tears blinded her, and it was a minute before she could put herself to rights and take the dress in question from the wardrobe. With trembling hands, she held it up in front of Hilary. In the center of the gown, just below the bodice, was the dark print of an iron. Ophelia's chit of a maid had burned it!

"And it is my fault, Lady Hilary. I know that you must take it out of my wages. Marie said that was only proper and that I should hope that I don't lose my place because of it!" Here she gave way to another storm of tears, and Hilary put her arms around her.

"But of course you won't lose your place, Lucy, and I'm certainly not going to take it out of your wages.

In fact," she said, brightening, "perhaps I shall have the price of the gown taken from Marie's wages!"

"Would you dare to do that, my lady?" asked Lucy, awed by the idea. "They would all be so very angry, and I wouldn't want to cause more trouble for you."

Lucy might be young and inexperienced, but she was observant, and Hilary's treatment at the hands of the Brawleys had not escaped her.

"Nonsense!" said Hilary, feeling better by the minute.

Not only was she rid of the dreadful gown, but she would have the opportunity to carry the war into the enemy's territory. She had been far too passive in allowing the Brawley ladies to mistreat her. Her father had been right: she must assume an air of authority.

For the moment, she knew, the advantage lay with her because Mr. Brawley clearly wished for the marriage. All too soon she would have no bargaining power at all. In fact, she acknowledged to herself, she would undoubtedly pay dearly for what she was about to do. Nonetheless, she was determined to do it. If nothing else, it would make her feel better. Having never had any power in her life, she decided that she would take advantage of her moment. Lucy, like Jack, was her responsibility and could not fend for herself.

Briskly, Hilary walked to the bell cord beside her bed and pulled it several times. In a few minutes one of the upstairs maids appeared and Hilary told her to bring Marie immediately. Her mouth open, the maid departed in search of her.

"Yes, my lady?" murmured Marie, bobbing a curtsy as she entered. She was a pretty girl, dark-skinned with large dark eyes, and Hilary could see why she had renamed herself. And, although Marie was attractive, she was probably at least a little jealous of Lucy's delicate porcelain beauty. Lucy looked far more like a lady than did Marie or her mistress.

"I understand that you burned my gown today, Marie," said Hilary, gesturing toward the gown, which was lying on the bed.

Marie's gaze darted venomously toward Lucy, who stepped back behind Hilary. "Then she lied to you, my lady," she replied. "She burned it herself and is trying to blame it on me."

"Lucy does not lie to me," remarked Hilary, her tone final. Jack growled gently in response to her tone, emphasizing his disapproval of the situation. "I shall speak to Miss Brawley about having this taken from your wages."

Marie flounced toward the door, but before she could open it, Hilary said sharply, "I haven't said that you are dismissed!"

Marie turned and looked at her insolently. "Yes, my lady?" she said, her lip curling slightly.

"I understand that you have been making Lucy's life miserable belowstairs. I expect to hear no more about it. Do you understand me?"

Marie's lip curled even further, and Hilary watched in fascination. She was surprised the girl could even speak with it in such a position. "Yes, my lady," she replied, bobbing the briefest of curtsies.

"Good! Then you may go," returned Hilary, waving her hand in dismissal as she had seen Lady Werrington do.

As the door closed behind the maid, Lucy stared at her in awe. "I've never seen you behave like that before, Lady Hilary," she whispered.

Apart from her defense of Jack, Hilary had never seen herself behave like that either. She felt quite exhilarated, even when she thought about the inevitable confrontation with Ophelia the next day. Now she had the upper hand and, if she got her bluff in, she might keep it, at least for the moment. Amazingly enough, it was possible that her father's advice had been correct. She would do her best to act with an air of authority.

As it happened, she did not have to wait until the next day to hear Ophelia's opinion of the situation. In less time than it took to brush her hair before retiring, the door to Hilary's chamber opened unceremoniously and Ophelia stormed in.

"What do you mean by calling in my maid and giving her orders?" she demanded, her voice shaking with fury. She took a step toward Hilary, and Jack, resenting her tone and her threatening gesture, barked warningly and bared his white teeth, so that she stopped in her tracks, glaring at all three of them.

"I meant what I said to her," replied Hilary calmly, brushing her hair and staring at her own reflection in the glass as though there were nothing more important than this evening ritual. "Here, Lucy, one hundred more strokes, please," she said, holding out the brush toward the girl.

Lucy scuttled past the seething Ophelia and applied herself diligently to brushing the silken length of Hilary's silvery hair.

"Well, I shall not take any money from her wages!" retorted Ophelia. "How nonsensical of you to enter into a servant's fight and take sides!"

"Do you pay Marie's wages yourself, Miss Brawley, or does your brother pay them?"

Ophelia paused in her diatribe and stared at Hilary, who, catching her eye in the glass, looked back at her knowingly.

"Yes, that's just what I mean," observed Hilary, smiling. "You understand my point. I believe that Mr. Brawley will see the necessity of doing just that, once I have spoken with him."

The door slammed sharply as Ophelia left the room, and Lucy bounced in joy, patting Jack who was bouncing with her.

"How cleverly you handled her, my lady!" she exclaimed. "Why, you are equal to any of them!"

Hilary doubted this, understanding fully why Ophelia had given in to her, and she knew her advantage would not last. Once they had her safely married to Raymond Brawley, she would be made to pay the piper. Still, for the moment she was content with her work and would not worry about the future.

Tomorrow, she felt, would be soon enough to deal with the problems that tonight's actions had created.

Three

Strangely enough, Hilary went down to breakfast far more serenely than she had on other mornings, even though she knew that she would be walking into a hornets' nest. She still had a slight feeling of euphoria from her encounter the night before. For someone who had seldom asserted herself in any way, facing down Ophelia had been heady stuff indeed.

"I am astounded that you have the courage to come down to breakfast," announced Mrs. Brawley in the tone of one who has harbored a serpent in her bosom, as Hilary seated herself at the table. Her daughters were also present, and all were obviously ready to do battle. Ophelia fairly bristled, even though she was silent, and Deidre's dark brows almost met over her eyes, so intent was her scowl.

"Indeed?" responded Hilary coolly, indicating to the footman that she would accept a cup of chocolate. "Is there something wrong with the breakfast? It looks quite appetizing to me."

She noticed a slight twitch of amusement in the lips of the footman serving her. Unfortunately for him, so did Mrs. Brawley, and her arctic glance quickly froze his features into their usual impassive expression.

"You are aware, I am certain, Lady Hilary, that I refer to last night's disgraceful episode," Mrs. Brawley informed her gravely, measuring her words carefully to give them added weight. Her thin lips grew even thinner as she made this pronouncement.

"I am glad to hear that we agree that it was indeed a disgraceful episode," said Hilary, biting into a slice of buttered toast with appetite. "Should one of my servants behave in such a manner, I would not be able to hold up my head."

Hilary realized with satisfaction that she sounded for all the world as though she were accustomed to being in charge of a household of servants instead of having only Lucy, and her just for the past week.

Before Mrs. Brawley could marshall her forces and make another attack, Hilary continued blandly, still giving her attention to her toast, "Pray don't be embarrassed, however, Mrs. Brawley. Even in the best-run households, a servant can sometimes prove unruly. I am certain that with the proper training, Marie will make a passable maid."

This proved too much for Ophelia, who could no longer wait for her mother to respond.

"This is not about Marie, Lady Hilary!" she began, her voice shrill.

"Indeed?" cut in Hilary deftly before she could continue. "I must admit that I am astonished—but gratified—Miss Brawley, that you have chosen to apologize for your own behavior."

"I, apologize?" gasped Ophelia, momentarily robbed of breath by Hilary's audacity. *"I* have nothing for which to reproach myself, Lady Hilary. *You* are the one who has behaved outrageously by giving orders to my servant and behaving as though you are mistress of this house already!"

A momentary silence fell over the table as they all considered what she had just said—for soon enough she would be mistress of the household, at least in name—but Ophelia continued to glare at Hilary defiantly.

After the pause had extended long enough for the others to become uncomfortable, Hilary said slowly, "I must tell you, Miss Brawley, that I am amazed that you do not see that I was simply taking care of my own affairs. It was, you see, *my* gown that was destroyed, not yours. And it was done by *your* servant, not mine—although I admit that Marie did it to attempt to have me give Lucy her notice. She has certainly been making my maid's life miserable belowstairs, and that, I feel, gives me a personal interest in the matter. I will not tolerate any further mistreatment of Lucy."

"*You* will not tolerate it!" gasped Mrs. Brawley, before her daughter could respond. "You dare to take that tone in the house where you are a guest, ma'am?"

Hilary's calm blue eyes met her sharp dark ones implacably. "I do indeed, Mrs. Brawley, for Lucy *is* my business, whether I marry your son or not."

This quiet reminder of how distressed Mr. Brawley would be should Hilary decide to withdraw from the match silenced them for the moment, but it was a silence that seethed through the day. Hilary escaped most of it, however, taking Jack and heading out again for a happy ramble over the grounds.

She returned in time to dress for dinner, grateful that she need no longer consider wearing the hideous mustard gown. If Marie were going to destroy something of hers, she had certainly chosen well. Hilary did not have to encounter the Brawley ladies in close quarters again until they gathered in the drawing room before dinner.

Fortunately for Hilary, Mr. Brawley had been closeted in the library with his man of business most of the day, so he had not yet had the opportunity to hear the complaints of his mother and sisters. Being a self-important man, he chose to regale them with his experiences during his two days away from them, certain that they must be as eager to hear as he was to tell.

As she drowsed gently in her chair, Hilary reminded herself that this was what she had to look forward to and that she might as well grow accustomed to it now. It was with considerable effort that she gave Mr. Brawley her complete attention.

Just as she managed to focus on him, however, Rutgers entered to announce that they had callers. They all looked up in surprise.

"Lady Carhill and Lord Grayden!" he trumpeted, pleased to have someone of consequence to announce. Lily, her vivid brunette beauty accentuated by a traveling dress the color of buttercups, stood smiling in the doorway. Behind her was a tall man, dark-haired and dark-eyed like Lily, who bowed to the assembled ladies.

Astonishment took the place of surprise for all concerned. While Lord Grayden was introducing himself to Mr. Brawley, Lily bore down on Hilary and embraced her.

"My *dearest* Hilary!" she exclaimed, her voice vibrant with emotion. Part of it was genuine, Hilary knew, but Lily enjoyed nothing more than putting on a show, and she proceeded to do so in grand style.

"I cannot apologize to you deeply enough, ma'am," Lily said, turning to Mrs. Brawley, who looked deeply gratified to receive an apology from such a person, although uncertain of the reason for it. "Not for the world would I have intruded upon you without notice, but when we drove into Templeton, I realized that we must be near Drake Hall. I simply could not come this close to my dearest Hilary without coming to see her!"

Here Lily turned again to her dearest Hilary, winked, and hugged her.

"Nonsense, Lady Carhill, I assure you it is no intrusion. It is an honor to have you and Lord Grayden grace our poor home," Mr. Brawley assured her pompously, pleased at the opportunity to refer to the imposing Drake Hall as his "poor home."

His mother, a little put out that he had answered for her, added sincerely, "We would be delighted to have you stay for dinner, Lady Carhill. And of course you must stay the night with us."

She turned to Rutgers, who still hovered near the door, and instructed him to inform Cook that there would be two more for supper and that two guest chambers should be prepared immediately.

"You are too gracious, ma'am!" exclaimed Lily, taking the hand of her hostess impetuously.

Hilary watched the scene with amusement. Lily still had her habit of speaking in exclamation points, and she had not lost her ability to take charge of a situation. Watching her in motion was like watching a force of nature.

She accompanied Lily to her chamber, and as soon

as the door had closed behind them, Hilary pounced upon her and hugged her.

"How wonderful of you to come, Lily!" she exclaimed. "I didn't think I would get to see you again for years and years. Once I marry Mr. Brawley, I shall be buried here forever!"

"Nonsense!" retorted Lily briskly, removing her hat and stripping off her gloves. "You shall not marry that man and his terrible family. I am going to free you!"

For a moment Hilary felt her hopes rise, but then she sighed and shook her head. "I appreciate it, Lily, but there's simply no way around it, I fear. My father needs the money that Mr. Brawley will give him as a settlement."

"Other men have money," returned Lily practically. "You need not marry such a man as this Brawley."

Hilary laughed. "Not all of us have men flinging marriage offers at our heads, Lily! He is the only one who has offered for me, and my father wishes for me to accept him."

"Men, bah!" Lily sniffed indignantly, dismissing the male portion of the population with a wave of her hand. "You need not do this if you don't wish to. I shall find you a husband if you truly want one, and I shall surely choose a better one than this Brawley."

Hilary laughed again, but more reluctantly this time. She knew her father would never approve crying off from the marriage. He had immediate plans for the money that Brawley would provide when the wedding took place. Once more she shook her head.

"I can't," she replied simply.

Lily took both her hands and looked into her eyes. Since Hilary was seated, this was easier than it would usually be, for she was a full head taller than her friend.

"I think you are wrong," she said, her voice serious for once, "but even if you must marry him, you shall have one last taste of happiness. Grayden and I have come to take you away to London. You shall have a last holiday at least."

"Lily! I can't just announce that I'm going to London on holiday when I am here to visit them!" she exclaimed, looking at her friend as though she had run mad.

"Naturally not! Do not fret about it, for I shall take care of it. Plan to leave tomorrow morning, however. We shall have a marvelous time!"

Lily gave her a ferocious hug. "I shall join you downstairs in just a few minutes," she said. "And in the meantime, do not let these terrible people distress you."

Still bemused by the turn of events, Hilary was closing the door gently behind her when she realized that Jack had not followed her into Lily's chamber. Starting back downstairs, she had just gained the landing when she saw him lying in the large marble entry hall, close to the doors of the drawing room. He caught sight of her at the same moment and rose to his feet, his tail wagging briskly. However, just as he trotted toward her, Mr. Brawley strode from the drawing room and tripped over him.

"Damned dog!" he exclaimed, regaining his balance with some difficulty. "Always underfoot!"

As he aimed his foot at Jack to kick him out of the way, Lord Grayden's hand clamped down upon his shoulder and jerked him back, throwing him off balance and giving Jack a chance to escape. The small terrier promptly took the opportunity, racing up the stairs with a yip of indignation.

His face scarlet, Mr. Brawley turned to glare at his guest, who had followed him from the drawing room, and Grayden met his eyes, unperturbed. There was a brief silence before Grayden spoke.

"I trust that you'll forgive my not being in full dress for dinner," he said calmly, gesturing to the travel dress he was still wearing. "I'm afraid that removing the dust of the road is all that I will be able to do. My valet has gone on ahead with my gear."

On ahead to where, Hilary found herself wondering as she withdrew behind a carved screen on the landing to avoid being seen. According to Lily, they had been on their way directly to Drake Hall to rescue her. Lord Grayden, she decided, must be as apt at deception as Lily.

"Of course not," mumbled Brawley with a forced graciousness. "I'll take you to your chamber myself. We do not stand on ceremony here."

Which was false, Hilary reflected in disgust. As false as anything possibly could be. The Brawleys were never nonchalant about matters of form as Lord Grayden had just been, or even as her father occasionally was. They stood upon ceremony with the relentlessness of those who hungered for the sort of life they perceived the members of the *ton* to live.

Still wishing to avoid being seen, she moved swiftly from the landing and up the steps, Jack now in her arms. Behind her she could hear them coming.

She hurried to her own chamber, leaving the door ajar so that she could watch them pass by.

Two more different men could not be found. Mr. Brawley's walk reminded her of a small rooster on the strut, while Lord Grayden's was the easy stride of a man accustomed to the outdoors. Tall though she was, Lord Grayden was taller. Even in his riding clothes he looked far more elegant than Mr. Brawley in his evening attire; Grayden's dark good looks were striking and his manner polished, while Mr. Brawley's looks were highly forgettable and his attitude arrogant.

She sighed as she picked up Jack and started down the stairs. As always, good fortune had smiled upon Lily. To have a man such as Lord Grayden as her cicisbeo was a feather in her cap indeed.

She mused for a moment. If Grayden were a feather in the cap, and doubtless an eagle feather, what would that make Mr. Brawley? she wondered. Hilary smiled to herself, amused by the sudden vision of a feather plucked from a scrawny, rain-soaked rooster. That, she felt, properly captured the essence of Mr. Brawley.

Four

Dinner that evening was a success only because of the efforts of Lady Carhill, occasionally assisted by Lord Grayden. Hilary did not feel inclined to talk, but she enjoyed hearing Lily's stories of Europe and watching the faces of the Brawleys, which radiated envy, pleasure, and pride by turns. Seldom had she had such an entertaining opportunity to study several people undergoing a range of emotions. Her fingers fairly itched for her pencils and pad of drawing paper.

"And as we returned home, Prinny himself said—" Lily was saying, causing the Brawley assemblage to sit straighter at the mention of the name.

"Do you know the Prince Regent?" demanded Ophelia in awe. "Is he as outrageous as they say he is?"

"Well, naturally he is," replied Lily, her dainty brows arched in surprise. "Everyone knows it. He has been so all his life."

"And does he actually wear a corset?" persisted Ophelia.

Lily clearly considered the question in poor taste, for her nose wrinkled fastidiously and she turned to Hilary.

"Do you still have the silver earrings I gave you?" she asked her friend, and Hilary nodded, smiling.

"Good! I bought you a bracelet to match when I was

in Rome. Grayden helped me to pick it out, did you not?"

Lord Grayden inclined his head slightly. "I was at least present at its purchase, ma'am," he said coolly to Hilary. "I cannot honestly say that I helped to pick it out. Lady Carhill is very particular in her taste."

"So I am!" agreed Lily. "That is why I spend so much of my time with you, my lord." And she dimpled prettily at him.

"And Lord Carhill? How does Lord Carhill spend his time?" inquired Mr. Brawley, appearing to take exception to being left out of the conversation. Lily had devoted herself to him during the first course, and he did not care to have her attentions diverted.

If Lily thought Mr. Brawley presumptuous—which she did—she covered it nicely, and shook her head.

"He spends his time largely with his doctors and his books. I am afraid that my husband is in rather poor health," she said sadly. "He has been so for some months now, which is why he is so grateful to have Grayden escort me everywhere."

If Mr. Brawley felt that she should have been at her husband's side instead of gadding about with a handsome young lord, he at least had the good sense not to say so aloud. And it was clear to Hilary that the feminine contingent of the Brawleys—even Mrs. Brawley—was entirely smitten by Lord Grayden. Just why this should be so, she was less certain of, for he had assuredly not attempted to charm them. Perhaps, Hilary thought, it was simply the sharp contrast between him and Mr. Brawley.

Lord Grayden suddenly caught her eye across the table and said, "I found a sketchbook on a table outside my chamber which your maid told me belongs to you, Lady Hilary."

Flushing a little, Hilary thanked him, hoping that

Lucy had retrieved it before Grayden had had an opportunity to look at it. The book contained sketches of the countryside, but it also contained some very telling caricatures of the people seated at the table with them. It had been unforgivably careless of her to leave it there. She had had her arms full and had stopped to pick up Jack, forgetting that she had laid it down for a moment.

"I can't imagine why anyone would bother making silly little drawings. Quite a waste of time, if you ask me," commented Ophelia, volunteering an opinion that no one had requested.

"I'm afraid that I would have to disagree with you, Miss Brawley," replied Lord Grayden. "Particularly when the artist is as gifted as Lady Hilary."

Her eyes flew to his face, and she saw that his expression was perfectly serious, though his manner was as politely distant as it had been all evening.

"Thank you, sir," she replied. "Do you draw?"

"Not nearly as well as you do, ma'am," he said, raising his glass in a mock salute. He had looked at them all, she was certain of it. His knowing expression as he toasted her convinced her. She would rip the offending pages from the sketchbook and burn them tonight.

"Well, I'm certain that there must be more interesting things to talk about," said Ophelia crossly, weary of a conversation that neither entertained her nor included her.

"Forgive me, Miss Brawley," said Lord Grayden, turning to her. "I see that you do not care for sketching. Do tell me about your interests. For instance, do you ride?"

Hilary froze, horrified by his seemingly innocent question. One of her sketches had been of Ophelia sitting in a mud puddle after being pitched off her horse. She retired briefly behind her napkin to regain her composure and when she emerged, she caught Lord Grayden's eye and frowned. His response was an arched eyebrow and another question for Ophelia.

"Or, perhaps, ma'am, you enjoy gardening?"

"Gardening?" replied Ophelia, astonished. "What would make you think that I would enjoy such a thing as that? Riding I adore, of course, because it is a necessary accomplishment for a lady, but gardening?"

"My error, Miss Brawley, forgive me. Perhaps I thought of it because I associated you with flowers."

Ophelia preened, accepting the implied tribute, but Hilary had difficulty retaining the composure she had just regained. Another of her sketches was of "Mistress Mary, quite contrary," and the face was unmistakably Ophelia's, wearing the sourest of expressions. She hoped that dinner would soon be over, or the dratted man would make reference to every caricature in the sketchbook.

When the ladies retired to the drawing room after dinner, Lord Grayden declined the traditional brandy and cigars with Mr. Brawley in the dining room.

"After all," he observed, bowing to the ladies, "there are far more ladies than gentlemen this evening, and I see no reason to deprive ourselves of their company for any longer than necessary."

The ladies appeared to be quite in agreement, although Hilary would have been happier to have him safely penned with Mr. Brawley for a while. The chief difficulty the others encountered in the drawing room was that only two ladies could sit beside Lord Grayden—and Ophelia and Deidre were swift. The others had to be content to sit at a greater distance while the two girls—or actually Ophelia, who dominated her sister in this as she did in all other things—monopolized his attention.

Hilary was relieved to be seated far enough away so that she could see all the actors in the play and not

participate actively—and she devoutly hoped he had
finished with his references to the sketches. Lily obviously wished to spend her time with Grayden, but she
sat apart and made occasional desultory conversation
with the others. Mrs. Brawley, however, was fully as
infatuated as her daughters, and gave her attention entirely to Lord Grayden, able to break away only when
Lily spoke directly to her. It annoyed Hilary to see their
behavior despite the fact that he was doing nothing to
ingratiate himself with them. He was courteous when
spoken to but cool, yet they were fascinated and made
no secret of the fact.

Not until Ophelia decided to play for them was there
an opportunity for anyone other than her to say a word
to him, and even then she patted the bench beside her,
hopeful that he would come and turn the music for her.
As he took his place, too well mannered to do otherwise, he glanced at Hilary, and she winced. Another of
her caricatures had been of Ophelia at the pianoforte,
and it had not flattered her abilities.

Grayden was kept so occupied that it was not until
they were breaking up the party to retire for the evening
and Lily had engaged the attention of the Brawleys
exclaiming over a portrait of the family that Hilary had
the opportunity to speak to him privately. The matter
of Jack had been weighing heavily on her mind. Even
though she hated the thought that he might classify her
as another female longing for his attention—or, worse
yet, refer to the sketchbook again—she felt obligated
to speak.

"I wanted to thank you, Lord Grayden, for protecting
my dog from being kicked this evening," she said in a
low voice. "It was very kind of you."

"Not at all, ma'am," he returned, bowing. "I would
have done the same for anyone. I do not like to see
animals mistreated. I was wondering, though," he con-

tinued, "if I might be able to borrow your sketchbook to entertain myself with for rest of the evening." His expression had not changed, but amusement glimmered in his dark eyes.

She attempted to glare at him, but her lips quivered. Clara was the only other person who had ever seen her drawings, and it was pleasant to know that someone else enjoyed them. "You were beastly," she said, giving way to a reluctant smile. "You might have given me away with your wicked comments."

"Of course I would not give you away," he responded. "You must remember that Lady Carhill has brought me here on your behalf. I was interested to see how deft your sketches were. By the time your maid wrenched the book away from me, I felt as though I knew the family intimately."

"It was very kind of you and Lady Carhill to come. I do appreciate the opportunity to see her again, although I think I will not be able to leave Drake Hall with you as she plans."

"Then you underestimate Lady Carhill, ma'am," he replied. "Having had some exposure to the lady, I feel that you may well be leaving with us. I, for instance, thought that I was accompanying her to Lord Carhill's estate, and so I sent my valet ahead of us. I did not know that I was coming here and then returning to London."

Hilary looked at him in dismay, but he did not appear angered by what had happened. "I do apologize, Lord Grayden, that—"

He held up his hand to stop her. "There is no need for you to apologize, ma'am. Lady Carhill merely wanted to ensure my agreement to this plan. No fault lies with you."

Lily came up and slipped her arm through his, winking at Hilary. "Be certain to get some rest tonight, my dear," she said. "You don't look as though you feel quite well. Have you got the headache?"

Hilary looked at her blankly for a moment, then responded quickly as she understood. "Just a bit," she confessed for the benefit of Ophelia and Mrs. Brawley, who had joined them. "Perhaps if I drink a tisane before bed, it will help."

"Just the thing," agreed Lily. "I'll look in upon you before I go to bed. We shall be leaving the first thing tomorrow, and I should hate for you not to be well enough to see us off."

"Oh, you need not leave so soon, Lady Carhill. Please do stay over a day or two," pleaded Ophelia, looking at Lord Grayden as she spoke.

"I'm afraid we are not able to," responded Lily, "but it is most kind of you to invite us. Come along, Grayden," she continued, turning toward the stairs. "And I shall be in shortly to see you, Hilary."

And Lily was as good as her word. A soft knock took Lucy to the door and Hilary dismissed her for the evening, telling the maid that she would need her early the next morning.

"I'm certain that I shall see the dreadful Miss Brawley on my way back to my chamber," Lily whispered as she closed the door behind Lucy. "I believe she is waiting in a spare room down the hall with the door open just a crack so that she can pretend to run into me as I leave. I shall tell her that I am most concerned about you. Rest assured that I shall have you out of here tomorrow morning. Just look ill when you come down to breakfast."

Before she could leave, Hilary said quickly, "Lily, I feel guilty that you kidnapped poor Lord Grayden in order to help me."

"Don't worry about Grayden, my dear. He does not really mind anything that I do, but I knew that if I told him I was bringing him into the home of a—forgive me, Hilary—of a family like the Brawleys, he might have resisted, and I wanted to rescue you immediately."

She gave Hilary a quick hug. "I must go now. If I leave Miss Brawley lingering too long, she may find an excuse to knock on poor Grayden's door."

When Hilary entered the breakfast room the next morning, she did her best to look ill. Lily was already present, and she had been at work.

"Oh, my dear," she said sympathetically. "Do come and sit down. I know that you can't eat anything because of your tooth, but perhaps you can force down a little tea."

Hilary, who was hungry, was inclined to think poorly of her friend's ruse at first, but she had not given Lily enough credit.

Turning to Mr. Brawley, Lily impetuously took his hand and looked into his eyes. "Mr. Brawley, much as I hate to rob you of dear Hilary's company, I am certain that I must take her back to London to have my surgeon look at her tooth. I have told Grayden that we must alter our plans."

Mr. Brawley stared at her, his cup halfway to his mouth. Hilary found it difficult to tell which astonished him more: Lily's request to take her to London or the fact that Lady Carhill was holding his hand.

Taking advantage of his momentary silence, Lily continued, "She has always been susceptible to infections, and I fear that this one is upon the brink of becoming a raging one. She is already running a fever."

"Nonsense!" exclaimed Mrs. Brawley stoutly. "Lady Hilary can have her tooth drawn here. There's no need at all for her to gad off to London. Why should you have to delay your own trip to return to Town?"

Mrs. Brawley appeared to be taking Lady Carhill's interest in Hilary quite personally.

"Grayden and I have agreed that we must delay it on Hilary's behalf. You must believe me when I say that I know her health better than you, ma'am. Why, I have seen these small indispositions turn into raging fevers in a matter of hours," replied Lily, twisting the truth without batting an eyelash. She squeezed Mr. Brawley's hand, which she was still holding. "And I know that you, Mr. Brawley, wish only what is best for her."

"Well, naturally I—" he began, but she gave him no more opportunity to speak.

"Wonderful!" she exclaimed. "Grayden and I shall make her comfortable in our carriage and return her to London immediately. She shall stay with me and Lord Carhill, and when she is herself again, I shall notify you so that you may come to fetch her."

"Fetch her?" repeated Mr. Brawley, looking mildly dazed. Lily frequently had that effect on people.

"Well, I had thought perhaps you—and your family, of course," she added, nodding at the ladies, "might wish to come to London to fetch Hilary when she is completely well again. Attending a party or two while you are there would help me to repay you for your kind hospitality."

The rest of the table sat stunned. Ophelia was the first to speak. "London! But, of course, Lady Hilary *must* go with you! We wouldn't wish her to be in ill health because we were lacking in any attention to her, would we, Raymond?" she asked, turning eagerly to her brother.

Deidre chimed in immediately. "Yes, do say we can go, Raymond! Just think of it! Why, we would be able to see Lord—that is, we would be able to see Lady Carhill once more!"

Lily paused a moment, then said, "I could, of course, simply send Hilary home in my carriage if coming to London is inconvenient for you, Mr. Brawley."

"Raymond!" scolded his sisters, each eager to convince him. "Tell her we will come!"

The final word was delivered by Mrs. Brawley. "Of course we will come to London, Lady Carhill. I would not wish it said that my family did not make every effort on Lady Hilary's behalf."

"Thank you, ma'am," said Lily quietly, but her eyes were dancing. Hilary was relieved to see that she at least did not allow herself a wink.

Across the table she caught Lord Grayden's dark eyes, expecting them once again to be alight with amusement; she was surprised by his quizzical expression. Doubtless he was amused by Lily's antics, Hilary thought, but why should he look at her in such a searching manner? When she glanced up again, he was still looking at her and she glanced away quickly, though not before her color rose.

Five

They finally managed to part from the Brawleys, tucking Hilary, Lucy, and Jack into the carriage and treating Hilary as though she were made of porcelain. Lily insisted upon a pillow, a hot brick for Hilary's feet despite the fact it was a sunny autumn day, and clove oil for her tooth. Eager to appear interested, their hosts supplied everything immediately and began to improvise additions of their own, including a bone for Jack and a volume of sermons for Hilary to peruse during her recovery. As the carriage eventually swept down the drive, all of the Brawleys stood in front of Drake Hall, the ladies waving their handkerchiefs in a final farewell.

Lily fell back against the cushions in exhaustion. "I did not think that they were going to be able to part with you," she said to Hilary, holding her temples as though they were throbbing. "If we had had to wait for them to bring out anything else, I should have shrieked in despair."

"Well, you started it, Lily," remarked Hilary cheerfully. "If you hadn't made me appear such an invalid and made so many demands of them, they wouldn't have had us wait while the cook prepared a basket. They merely wished to impress you with how attentive they are."

Jack was presently guarding the basket, having noticed that there were interesting aromas emanating from it. His chin rested gently on the straw handle and his dark eyes regarded Hilary hopefully.

"I did not expect such a dustup, though," complained her friend. "I simply wanted them to understand that your condition was to be taken seriously, not that I expected to place you in hospital immediately upon arriving in London. Which, of course, I shall have to do now," she added mischievously. "Grayden and I shall escort you directly there, never mind going home with me."

"That is the greatest amount of attention I have received in that household," observed Hilary thoughtfully, ignoring Lily. "Of course, I know that it wasn't for me. It was for you and for Lord Grayden."

She paused and looked at Lily in admiration. "I would not have thought that you could have managed my escape so nicely, you know. I didn't think that you had a chance of succeeding."

"I always succeed, do I not, dear Grayden?" she asked, turning and patting his cheek playfully.

Grayden glanced down at her, then across at Hilary and nodded ruefully. "I believe that we may safely say, Lady Hilary, that she is quite correct in her statement. I have never failed to see her get what she wants, whether it is wise for her to have it or not."

Hilary smiled, but she wondered whether he was referring to taking her to London with them. Why would Lord Grayden think that was not wise? She knew from the curious expression she had seen on his face at breakfast that something was perturbing him, though she did not know him well enough to guess what it might be.

Deciding that thinking about that was fruitless, she gave her attention to the passing countryside as Lily went to sleep with her head on Grayden's shoulder. She could not do other than love Lily, particularly when she had gone to such trouble on her behalf, but it did occur to her that life seemed more unjust than usual. Lord Grayden had been right: Lily always got what she wanted.

Having never in her life gotten what she wanted, except for Jack, Hilary could not imagine what that might feel like. In fact, she was not even certain what she would want if she had a choice. She thought for a moment of Werrington Manor and knew immediately that she did not want to go home. She thought of Drake Hall and knew that she never wished to go back there again, even though it was inevitable. Sighing, she decided that it was better not to think about what one wanted when there were no options.

"What are you thinking about, Lady Hilary?" asked Grayden. Lily was now soundly asleep, and Lucy had helped him to settle her more comfortably, tucking a lap robe about her as she continued to lean against him. Lucy herself now slumbered peacefully next to her mistress, and Jack slumbered gently next to the lunch basket.

Hilary was caught fairly off-guard. Aside from Clara, and occasionally Lily during the brief time they had been together, no one in her life had ever asked her such a question. She was accustomed to the privacy of her thoughts simply because no one was interested in them.

"I was thinking of what you said about Lily," she replied honestly.

"And what was that?" he asked.

"That she always gets what she wants. That's most extraordinary, you know."

"Well, it *is* unusual *always* to get what one wants, but I don't know that I would say that it is extraordinary," he said, after considering the matter for a moment.

"That, sir, is because you are who you are," Hilary said crisply. "If you were a single woman with no dowry and whose face was not her fortune, you would realize that having *any* of the things one wants is the most extraordinary good fortune imaginable."

"You amaze me, Lady Hilary," he returned. "I know that you are a single woman, and perhaps it may be true that you have not a dowry, but most certainly you should have realized that your face *is* your fortune."

Hilary stared at him for a moment, suspecting mockery, but she could detect none. His expression remained serious, and she decided she must make the situation clear.

"I have had two Seasons in London, Lord Grayden, and I did not take," she said briefly, determined to show him that she understood her own shortcomings. "Mr. Brawley was so kind as to make a bid on me at the close of my second Season."

Before he could respond, she added sharply, "And allow me to point out, sir, that even if my face *were* my fortune—and I have ample evidence to the contrary—I would still not be in your position."

"And what is my position, Lady Hilary?" he asked quietly. "Precisely how do you perceive it?"

Hilary hesitated, then plunged. "It seems to me, Lord Grayden, that you are able to do very much as you please. You are a man of means, and your time is your own—unless, as it appears, you choose to place it at Lady Carhill's command. And it really does not matter what you choose to do with your time. The point is that you *may* choose. That makes your position very different from my own. Like most women, I must obey first my father and then my husband, should I marry. Those are my choices. You have no such constraints."

He nodded briefly. "I confess, Lady Hilary, that I had not thought of things in just that manner. Although I believe that you overstate my freedom and your own restrictions, I see that ours are still very different situations. I apologize."

She inclined her head to acknowledge his apology. There was a brief silence, then Grayden added matter-of-factly, "But your face is your fortune, Lady Hilary, say what you will."

Hilary began to bristle, but before she could reply, he continued. "And I do not refer to mere prettiness. I mean that your face shows your character instead of concealing it. There are laugh lines around your eyes, and your mouth curves upward when your features are at rest. Your eyes are kind—except when you are angry, of course, as you were just now—and intelligent. So you see, Lady Hilary, your face is indeed your fortune."

"You appear to be a student of faces, Lord Grayden," she replied after a brief silence.

"As you are, ma'am," he replied, bowing.

She was unsure just how she should respond to his comment. Certainly he was not flirting; he had just assured her that she had an interesting face, not a pretty one. She was not offended by that, for she had no illusions about her beauty. He had seemed to speak quite seriously, so she was equally direct, which was her natural manner.

"I thought that I concealed my emotions more effectively," she said finally. "I had no idea that my face was such an open book."

"You are transparent," he agreed. "You don't hide behind a facade. You don't playact. You are who you are."

"Except when I must pretend to have the toothache, of course," she said, smiling, hoping to give the conversation a lighter note.

"Except then, of course," he agreed. "As soon as we are in London, I will take you straightaway to the best surgeon I know. He will pull a tooth for you and put your mind at rest for not telling the Brawleys the truth."

"How did you know that was troubling me?" she asked, surprised. Little though she liked the Brawleys, it always bothered her to speak something other than the truth.

"It was not difficult to guess," he responded. "It was written on your face."

Hilary studied him for a moment, and he asked, smiling a little, "And do you read my character in my face, ma'am?"

She considered the question a moment, then shook her head. "I don't believe you reveal very many of your thoughts, Lord Grayden," she responded slowly. "I can see when you are amused, as you were at dinner last night when you brought up my sketchbook, but I cannot often tell what your reactions are otherwise."

"Ah, the sketchbook," he murmured. "I trust that your maid packed that carefully for you so that it does not fall into the wrong hands."

"I packed it myself, sir," she assured him crisply. "After the things you said, I greatly feared that it might be seen. I burned the most offensive of the sketches last night."

"That is a pity," he replied, his tone sincere. "I meant it when I said you are quite gifted, you know. I greatly enjoyed your work."

"Yes, well, I'm afraid that Ophelia and her family might not be quite as amused as you are. And I am going to be a member of their family, so I decided that I had best not wound them. After all, I did not draw the pictures to hurt anyone, merely to make myself feel better."

"And did you feel better after drawing them?" he asked curiously.

She smiled. "Oh, yes. That has always relieved my feelings tremendously. It is as though putting down on paper what is troubling me relieves me of the pain of it. It is an antidote for unhappiness."

He stared out the window for a moment as the carriage rattled on. "And are you often unhappy, Lady Hilary?" he asked finally.

She shook her head. "As seldom as I can manage. Unhappiness is not profitable. It is not even self-indulgent," she observed. "After all, I damage myself more than anyone else if I sink into despair. I may not be able to control what happens to me, but I can control my reactions to those things. Why not learn to find amusement in the pleasures that are available to me?"

"Why not, indeed?" he murmured.

That appeared to be the close of the conversation, and Hilary gave herself up to watching the changing scenery outside the window, enjoying the sight of a flock of sheep in a meadow and the small boy standing with them. The urchin took off his hat and waved it, and Hilary waved back at him.

"Have you no one who is interested in whether you are unhappy?" Lord Grayden asked abruptly.

Startled by his question, Hilary shook her head.

"What of your family?"

She shrugged and smiled ruefully. "My father wishes me to marry well," she replied lightly. "He and my stepmother have five sons to provide for, so my responsibility is clear."

"And he considers a marriage to Mr. Brawley 'marrying well,'?" asked Grayden, a slight sharpness in his tone.

Hilary nodded. "Mr. Brawley is a very wealthy

man," she replied simply, returning her gaze to the passing scene offered by the window.

"I see."

Finding the conversation somewhat disquieting since she did not care to air her dirty linen in public, Hilary closed her eyes and feigned sleep. She was flattered by his interest but revealing such private matters to a relative stranger—even a very attractive one so closely attached to her good friend—was unsettling.

Fortunately, there was no more private conversation between them. When they stopped at a posting-house for refreshment, Lily and Lucy and Jack awakened; and as they neared London that evening, the conversation turned to what they would do in that city.

"I would like to visit the bookshops and the theater—and Ackermann's," said Hilary in response to Lily's questions.

Lily dismissed these with a wave of her hand. "You are in urgent need of a wardrobe, my dear, and I will have my hairdresser come round immediately, too. I cannot think why you allowed them to dress you in such colors," she said, eying Hilary's bottle green traveling dress with active dislike.

"But, Lily, I cannot afford a—"

Lily leaned over and pressed her fingers against Hilary's lips. "But I can. Not another word. You mustn't rob me of my pleasures."

Hilary tried again. "Lily, I'll only be in London two or three days, so why—"

"Nonsense!" interrupted her friend. "You will be here at least a fortnight. I shall see to that. After all, we will need that long."

"We will need that long?" repeated Hilary, astonished. "For what?"

"We will need that long for me to find you a husband and free you of Mr. Brawley once and for all!"

Hilary's startled glance flew from Lily to Lord Grayden, who lifted his eyebrows and shrugged. "Well, Lady Hilary, you cannot say that you have not been warned," he said. "And you must remember that Lily always gets what she wants."

"But of course I do," that lady agreed complacently, tucking her arm through his and smiling.

Hilary glanced at Lucy, who had been taking all of this in with an open mouth. She looked fully as amazed as Hilary felt. When Hilary turned her attention back to the window, she saw that the heath had given way to city streets, and the lights of shop fronts were glowing in the twilight. Surreptitiously, Lucy gripped her hand as she had when they had approached Drake Hall. Once again they were entering a new world.

Six

And it was indeed a new world, reflected Hilary, looking round the chamber that had been prepared for her. A new world in every sense of the word.

When they arrived at Lord Carhill's home in Grosvenor Square, Hilary scarcely had a chance to catch her breath and settle Jack in his basket with his bone before Lily came to usher her into the presence of that gentleman. Hilary had protested, fearing that she would disturb him.

"Of course you will not disturb him!" Lily assured her. "I have told Robert all about you and he is looking forward to meeting you at last. He would be greatly distressed if I did not bring you to him."

Lord Carhill, although thirty years Lily's senior, was still a handsome man, his hair more gray than brown. He looked pale and his illness had, Lily had told her, caused him to be thinner. Still, his eyes were bright and alert, his manner cultivated and friendly. Hilary felt at ease immediately.

"I have heard a great deal about you, Lady Hilary," he assured her as she seated herself in a chair next to his. A pleasant fire crackled in the grate and Lord Carhill was swathed in a dressing gown of dark velvet. "Lady Carhill tells me that you are—I think her words were—'vastly clever but not at all a bluestocking.' "

Hilary flushed, for she knew all too well that being

called clever could be a death knell for a lady in society unless it referred to being witty, but he said it so kindly that she could not take offense.

"Lily is too kind to me, Lord Carhill," she replied. "I am afraid that she overrates my intelligence."

"But of course I don't overrate you at all, dearest girl!" responded Lily, who was sitting on the arm of her husband's chair. "She told me all about *Childe Harold* when it came out during our first Season, Robert," she added, patting her husband's arm, "or else I never would have had the least notion what Lord Byron was talking about."

Lord Carhill regarded his wife fondly. "No, I cannot say that you are fond of reading, my dear." Here he looked back at Hilary to include her in the conversation. "I can see that you are fortunate to have such a friend."

"Hilary is my counterpart, my complement, Robert," explained Lily very seriously. "She is clever, while I am not; she is serious where I am lively; she is tall and I short; she—"

"Yes, yes, I do get the idea, Lily," Lord Carhill interceded, noting the effect that the list was having upon their guest.

Although Lily appeared to be ascribing the positive characteristics to her friend, that was not the reality, as both he and Hilary were quick to realize. Whether the realization was quite as clear to Lily was another question, one that Hilary did not wish to examine closely.

"I hope, Lady Hilary," said Lord Carhill kindly, "that you will consider this your home for as long as you may wish. I am grateful that you are here. Things are too often very dull for my wife since I am not able to see to her amusement."

"I am excessively happy, Robert," Lily assured him, dropping a butterfly kiss upon his cheek as she stood up, "and not at all bored. Hilary and I will have a marvelous time and Grayden will be our squire until you are well again."

A shadow passed briefly across Lord Carhill's face, and Hilary wondered whether it was caused by the mention of Grayden or by the thought that he might not ever be well again. Lily had not indicated that, but Hilary could see that the man had been—and perhaps still was—gravely ill. The shadow passed quickly, however; and Lily, even if she were inclined to observe people closely, would have missed it since she was looking at Hilary.

"Ah, Grayden," murmured Lord Carhill. "And how is he faring in trying to keep pace with you, my dear?"

"He does very well, and he asked me to tell you that he will be in to pay his respects to you tomorrow morning, Robert."

"That is very kind of him," replied her husband. "Tell him that I shall look forward to it. Tell him, too, my dear, that Henry is in town once more."

Lily made a small grimace that Lord Carhill could not see. "Is he, indeed? I thought that he was to spend the month at Tommy Sanford's hunting box."

"So he was," he sighed, "but something apparently happened to cause him to change his plans."

"Well, I will tell Grayden that he has returned. And now we will let you rest, for I see that we have quite worn you to a thread."

And he did look suddenly weary, Hilary saw, and she regretted that they had tired him. As she stood, however, Lord Carhill took her hand and looked up at her.

"Thank you again for coming, Lady Hilary. Please do come in and see me. I am not always so quickly tired."

"Of course I will, sir," she assured him, returning

his smile. There was no doubt, she thought, that Lily had been very fortunate in her marriage, not merely because Lord Carhill was a wealthy, titled man, generous to a fault, nor because he was intelligent and kind. When his eyes rested upon Lily, his face lit up. He was, Hilary saw, a man very much in love with his wife.

She had no chance to remark on that to Lily, however, for they encountered a slender young man in evening dress just outside Lord Carhill's room.

"Your father is tired, Henry. You should not bother him now," she said, her voice sharp.

"Oh, I shall not be more than a moment, Lily—never fear." He looked at Hilary, and bowed. "But do introduce me to this vision of loveliness. Who is this Diana?"

Lily turned to her friend with an air of resignation. "Hilary, this is my husband's son, Lord Henry. You must try not to mind too much what he says. He fancies himself a heartbreaker."

The heartbreaker had already taken Hilary's hand and was bowing low over it.

"Henry, this is my dear friend, Lady Hilary Jamison. Do try to be on your best behavior with her."

"How could I be otherwise?" he asked, looking up— quite far—into Hilary's eyes. "Were I to offend the goddess, she would have only to take out one of her arrows and shoot me through the heart."

"Yes, well that sounds quite an admirable idea, Henry," Lily conceded briskly, hurrying Hilary along the passageway. Henry stood looking after them for a moment before entering his father's chamber.

"He is such a tiresome boy," complained Lily as she led Hilary back to her chamber. "He fancies himself a ladies' man, but I've yet to see any ladies making cakes of themselves because of him. I cannot see why he does not take a page from Grayden's book. Surely the contrast is sharp enough between them that even Henry can see it."

"I should think that the contrast between him and his own father would be even more striking," remarked Hilary, feeling that she should make an effort on Lord Carhill's behalf.

"Oh, of course Henry is nothing like Robert, and I know that Henry is a constant disappointment to him. But Grayden is much nearer Henry's own age. He wouldn't think to compare himself to his father."

Nor would you, Hilary thought, her heart going out to Lord Carhill.

She said nothing more on the subject, however. Lily opened the door to Hilary's chamber and instructed her to be ready as soon as possible, for they were going out. For the time being, Hilary had no time to think about anything or anyone else, so absorbed were she and Lucy in preparing for the excursion.

The remnant of the evening was spent in a trip to the theater. Lily did not intend to waste a minute of her guest's time in London, and Lord Grayden called for them as soon as Hilary had had time to change.

The gown she wore was, she well knew, far from flattering. She was tall and thin, and the vertical lines of the pattern of the material emphasized that, while its alternating stripes of yellow-green and snuff brown washed out her already pale skin and did nothing for her blue eyes and silver hair. It had, naturally, been made according to Lady Werrington's instructions. She felt as dowdy as that lady had intended her to feel, but she could not help the glow of excitement at doing something different.

She had hoped to see Edmund Kean playing in *Lear,* but they arrived in time for the second performance, which starred an opera-singer named Vestris as Macheath in *The Beggar's Opera.* The exceedingly attractive young woman appeared on stage in breeches, much to Hilary's astonishment.

"Yes, everyone talks of nothing but her legs," said Lily crossly, when Hilary remarked on the costume Vestris was wearing. "It is the most indelicate thing imaginable. I cannot think why the theater allows it."

"I believe we have only to look about us and we know the answer to that," responded Lord Grayden, who was seated on the other side of Lily in their box. "She is a tremendous success and will make Elliston a fortune."

"Yes, ever since that man became manager, taste has gone out the window," returned Lily, growing still more irritable.

"Perhaps taste has gone out the window, but assuredly money has come in," he answered.

Hilary glanced at the audience. What Lord Grayden said was obviously true. The theater was packed and the greater part of the audience appeared enraptured by Vestris. Lily was a marked exception, but then, Hilary reflected, Lily was not accustomed to sharing the limelight with anyone, not even an acclaimed performer.

"We will spend our evening more pleasantly tomorrow night," Lily assured her on the way home. "We shall be attending the Sheridans' ball."

"Thank you for tonight," said Hilary. "I enjoyed seeing Madame Vestris. Now I shall know what people are talking about when they refer to her."

Lily sniffed indignantly. "To be sure you will, but what a waste! She is completely vulgar. I cannot imagine why anyone would wish to speak of her."

"She has become famous for her breeches roles, Lily. You know that," remarked Grayden. "Why are you so out of reason cross about it tonight?"

"It was just tiresome, seeing everyone so mesmerized by that chit. Even you, Grayden, do not find fault with her. Why, she's only a silly girl!"

Grayden shrugged. "She may be only a silly girl, but she's a very successful one."

Hilary saw with misgiving that when he glanced at her, his eyes suddenly glinted with amusement. "Now, Lady Hilary, there's a possibility I should imagine you had not considered among your choices."

Hilary looked blank, and Lily even blanker.

"Whatever are you talking about, Grayden?" Lily demanded. "Do explain yourself more clearly."

"I merely meant, Lady Hilary," he explained, focusing his attention entirely on her instead of on Lily, "that you said you had few choices, but the stage is a choice I should imagine you did not consider."

"Hilary? Hilary go on the stage? Are you mad, Grayden? Whatever possessed you to say such an outrageous thing? What choices are you talking about?"

Seeing that Lily was growing genuinely annoyed, Hilary responded quickly, "No, I had not seriously considered the stage as a career, Lord Grayden. I believe that one is supposed to have talent before doing so."

"Did you not watch Vestris tonight?" retorted Lily. "A lack of talent assuredly did not keep her from performing."

"Well, even if you could not sing, Lady Hilary, I feel certain that you could play the breeches parts to perfection," said Lord Grayden.

"Grayden!" shrieked Lily, scandalized. "What a thing to say! Apologize to Hilary for making such a vulgar comment!"

Hilary, who had been somewhat taken aback by his words, was even more startled by the strength of Lily's reaction. "It doesn't bother me, Lily," she hastened to assure her friend. "Truly it does not."

Turning to Lord Grayden, she added, smiling, "I

shall promise to play a breeches role when you agree
to play the part of the lady, sir."

Grayden bowed. "I shall be at your service, ma'am,
whenever you are ready to do so. And I assure you that
I referred only to the fact that your form would allow
you to play the part of a youth."

"Oh, really!" pouted Lily. "There's no need to carry
on like this over one little comment, no matter how
unnecessary and tasteless it was, Grayden."

Hilary sighed. Perhaps it was not so very different
a world here after all. She hoped that Lily's behavior
was not going to be erratic during the entire visit. She
could feel her friend's irritation, and she had begun to
suspect that Lily's feeling for Lord Grayden might be
more than a passing fancy. She thought of Lily's poor
husband, loving her dearly and confined to his chamber, and shook her head.

"It is not a just world," she informed Jack before
going to bed. He and Lucy had remained closeted in
her chamber until her return, and Lucy had been fairly
shaking with excitement at the thought of being in London.

Jack regarded her with wistful eyes and shook his
tail tentatively, disturbed by her tone. She rubbed his
furry forehead fondly and then crawled into bed. At
least she had Jack, who loved her, and she would have
a few more days here before having to return to her
fate.

For a moment she thought of Lord Grayden's dark
eyes shining with amusement and sighed once more,
pulling the cover up over her head. There was no use
in even thinking of him, she reminded herself. He was
clearly staked as Lily's territory, and even if he were
not, it would do her no good. He was as far removed
from her as the stars. And, to cap it all off, he thought
that she could play the part of a man.

She was to marry Mr. Raymond Brawley. Lord Carhill was in love with Lily. Lily was in love with Grayden. Grayden was—Well, who knew what Grayden felt?

It was an unjust world.

Seven

As always, she felt better in the morning. Even if she were to have only a few days, she would make the most of each one. Today, she first had to meet with Frederic, who had come to take care of Lady Carhill's coiffure. Hilary had been turned over to him as an emergency problem to take in hand while Lily conferred with Madame DeLeon, her couturiere, over the abysmal state of her guest's wardrobe. As he examined the smooth coronet of braids that she normally wore, Frederic sniffed disdainfully.

"There is no choice, Lady Hilary," he announced. "We *must* cut your hair. I shall fix it so that you wear it in a little knot of curls, and pull the tendrils to frame the face so it is not so angular. Like this."

He loosened Hilary's hair so that it fell in a cascade of silver over her shoulders and whipped a sharp pair of scissors from his jacket pocket. Fingering a long strand, he prepared to make his artistic changes.

"No!" protested Hilary, who had been thrown off-balance by the quickness of his conversation and his movements.

"No?" he demanded, astonished. "Did you say no, madam?"

Hilary nodded violently and snatched the strand of hair from his fingers. "I wish to keep my hair long so that I may wear it as I always have."

"Then why," he asked indignantly, "did you wish for me to style your hair?"

"Lady Carhill wishes for me to have it cut," she explained, "and I should not mind having a few loose curls to frame my face, as you suggested. But I do not wish for you to cut the rest. I can see that what you say about the curls softening the angles of my face is true," she added, wishing to pacify him.

Somewhat mollified, he fingered a lock near her ear. "Yes, madam, I assure you it will make all the difference," he said, cutting and shaping deftly.

Hilary kept him under careful surveillance, fearful that his enthusiasm might carry him away so that she ended up with short curls all over her head. When he had finished, however, she was compelled to admit that he had known what he was doing. The coronet of braids was back in place, and the loose curls around her face and at the nape of her neck did much to make her look more delicate.

"Superb!" Frederic exclaimed as he regarded his handiwork. "Even with those atrocious plaits of hair, you look magnificent, madam! From the sow's ear, I have—"

Seeing Hilary's expression in the glass, he broke off hurriedly. "Forgive me, my lady. It is simply that my feelings ran away with me. I did not mean it, of course, except about your hair."

"Of course," Hilary agreed dryly. She stood up, her spirits somewhat dampened by his unfortunate comparison.

However, by the time Lucy had finished helping her dress for the ball that evening, Hilary's spirits had bubbled up once more. Lady Carhill's patronage had quickened the fingers of her couturiere, and the newly finished gown that Hilary was wearing was lovely, unlike anything she had ever had before.

"You look splendid, ma'am," breathed Lucy, straightening the blue silk skirt of the gown. The blue was as deep as her eyes, perfectly matched to them, and her complexion, now accentuated instead of washed out by the colors she was wearing, looked creamy against the cornflower blue. Her hair, no longer so old-fashioned and severe in its look, glowed against the blue.

The remarkable thing, thought Hilary, was that she *felt* splendid. Never before had she imagined there was the slightest possibility of her being considered a beauty. Now, however, fueled by Lucy's admiration, the thought began to nibble at the edges of her mind, and it was not unwelcome.

The thought received confirmation as soon as they arrived at the Sheridans' home. Every window glowed with candlelight and the number of vehicles made traffic impossible. They left their carriage some distance from the house so that they would not have to wait in the snarl, and Lord Grayden escorted them into the ballroom, presenting Hilary to their host and hostess.

A crowd gathered around Lily at once. It had been just the same at all the balls they had attended before she married, so Hilary was prepared for it. At one point, the crush around them grew so great that she tried to slip away. Lord Grayden, she noticed, stayed very close at hand, but she could see no reason to remain.

Lily saw her going, however, and called to her. When Hilary returned, Lily linked her arm firmly through her friend's, whispering, "It is just as it was when we first met, Hilary. We go excellently together. We offset one another in just the right way."

It was true that they were a decided contrast. As Lily had pointed out the night before, she was short while

Hilary was tall, lively while Hilary was serious. However, had Lord Carhill not cut her comparison short, she could have added that she was a striking brunette while Hilary was fair, she had a handsomely rounded figure while Hilary was tall and thin, she was beautiful while Hilary was decidely plain. And it was true, she thought. The contrast between them showed Lily to the greatest advantage possible.

Suddenly the crush of people seemed less amusing, the night less glowing. It was disheartening to think that this might have been the main reason for Lily's rescue of her. When Lily was distracted by a newcomer to the group and momentarily released her arm, Hilary took advantage of the opportunity and escaped to a far corner of the room.

To her surprise, she did not remain alone there for long. In a matter of minutes, she had gathered a few admirers of her own, beginning with Colonel Hague, a middle-aged gentleman freshly returned from India. It was difficult for Hilary to credit the thought that they *were* admirers, believing at first that perhaps the four men who joined her soon after the colonel had were companions and had merely stopped to be pleasant. When each of them wished to secure her hand for a dance, however, she began to believe that the evening might be more enjoyable than she had anticipated.

Colonel Hague proved to be a most interesting man, full of tales about his adventures in foreign parts; and Hilary, who wished to travel, hung on his every word. The other four, who were younger, were enjoyable companions. But none was as interesting as the colonel, and she sat down to refreshments with him.

As she danced with him a second time, she noticed Lord Grayden watching her, again with the same quizzical expression he had worn the morning Lily had duped the Brawleys into allowing her to come to Lon-

don. For a moment she was distressed, but then she
decided that she was being nonsensical. He might be
a student of character, but what he thought of her mat-
tered neither one way nor the other. Hilary straightened
her shoulders and gave herself over to the joys of the
dance and to at least one evening of being young and
attractive.

Later in the evening, Hilary saw to her dismay that
Lord Henry was threading his way across the room in
her direction. Remembering his comments to her the
night before, she was afraid that she might be his goal,
and her fear proved well founded. By the time he arrived, she still had not been able to think of a plausible
reason not to dance with him, for she was between
partners and Colonel Hague had just regretfully taken
his leave.

Lord Henry swept her a low bow and sighed soulfully as he looked into her eyes.

"You are a vision, Lady Hilary—or should I call you
Diana?" he murmured, lifting her hand to his lips.

"Do call me Lady Hilary. And I notice that you do
not say a vision of what, Lord Henry," she returned
lightly, trying to withdraw her hand.

"Why, of beauty, of course. That is what drew me
across the room, like a moth toward a candle flame.
Do say that you will give me the next dance."

"I'm sorry, Henry, but Lady Hilary is engaged for
the next one," replied Lord Grayden briskly. "The moth
had better find another candle flame."

Hilary looked round in relief. She hadn't heard him
walk up; and although his searching questions made
her a little uneasy, to be rescued from the dreadful
Henry was worth almost any price. Besides, she admitted to herself, she was pleased that he had sought her
out.

She managed to withdraw her hand, murmuring her

regrets to Henry as she took Lord Grayden's arm. Instead of leading her onto the dance floor, however, he walked with her onto the terrace. Despite the coolness of the evening, the air within had overheated because of the crush of the crowd, and the freshness outside— even in London—acted like a tonic. She was revived immediately.

"And so are you enjoying yourself as much as you had expected, Lady Hilary?" he inquired, leaning against the balustrade and looking down at her. He made no reference to Lord Henry.

How very odd it was, she thought, to be looking up at someone as she talked. Normally she had to look down, as she did with Lord Henry and Mr. Brawley. It had taken Miss Dunsmore a full year during her girlhood to train Hilary to remain standing straight instead of bending toward people as she spoke to them. So absorbed was she in this realization that he had to repeat his question.

"Oh, yes, indeed I am. It is all quite wonderful," she answered fervently.

"Quite like being Cinderella, isn't it?" he inquired dryly.

Hilary shrugged, annoyed by his tone. Suddenly the evening once again seemed less wonderful. Apparently it was going to be impossible to enjoy an evening of unalloyed pleasure.

"I suppose you could say so," she replied. "Only without the happy ending, of course. When the ball is over and the clock strikes twelve, I will be returned to the ashes and cinders at Drake Hall."

"Certainly it cannot be as bad as all that," he commented, studying her. "Drake Hall is a handsome establishment and, even if the Brawleys are not people of taste, you will at least have a comfortable life there."

"I fear that you are in no position, sir, to imagine

what life will be like for me there—nor do you know what I would consider a comfortable life. I believe we have already had a conversation very much like this," she returned, her gaze steady.

Changing the topic abruptly, he said, "You do know, don't you, that Lily is only using you?"

She had come to that realization, of course, but it was curiously disheartening to hear it from someone else, and particularly from this man. Hilary stared at him a moment, her hard-won assurance so recently acquired vanishing in a blink.

"What do you mean by that, Lord Grayden?" she asked, dreading to hear his reply. She could accept unpleasant truths about her own condition more gracefully when they were not so obvious to other people.

"You heard her tonight. She thinks that you make an excellent foil for her."

"You mean that she thinks she looks that much prettier because I am by her side for contrast," said Hilary without expression.

"Something like that," he agreed, in what she could only consider a most unchivalrous manner.

"Yet she has ordered me a new wardrobe and brought her own hairdresser in to attend me," observed Hilary slowly.

"I am aware of that, ma'am. I do not say that she holds you in dislike, and she is known now to be your sponsor. In her own mind, she could not do otherwise. It would be a reflection upon her. And too," he added, "I must be fair. In her own way, Lily is very fond of you."

"And so you think, sir, that Lily believes that even if I am, as you say, Cinderella for the moment, I am no threat to her? She believes that even when I am at my best, I serve only for contrast to her?"

He nodded. "I don't wish to offend you, Lady

Hilary," Grayden said, placing his hand upon her arm as though to comfort her, "but I have observed Lady Carhill closely enough to know that, even though she is, as I say, undoubtedly fond of you, her actions will nonetheless always be self-serving."

"Even if that is true, Lord Grayden," she said slowly, moving abruptly back from him, for both his touch and his words were disturbing, "I would prefer to have this life for a short time than not to have it at all."

"You're only the plaything of the moment," Grayden said brusquely, his eyes boring into hers. "She is like a child. She will drop you and forget you when she becomes bored."

"Even so," she repeated stubbornly, "better a little happiness than none at all."

Hilary turned away from him, not wishing even to think about the Brawleys now. She was attempting to have her only bit of amusement before the bleak years of being Mrs. Raymond Brawley began. Even if what Lord Grayden said of Lily was true—and honesty forced her to acknowledge that he might well be correct—she refused to let that disturb her. Lily at least had gone to the trouble of coming to Drake Hall to rescue her, which was more than anyone else had ever done for her.

As she returned to the ballroom, she found herself wishing that she could not still feel Grayden's hand upon her arm and see his eyes searching hers. She could be happier, she felt, if she were to see less of Lord Grayden. His effect upon her—in every way— was most unsettling.

Eight

When she joined Lily in the drawing room the next morning, she had already decided that she would concentrate as much as possible upon enjoying herself during the next few days. She would not allow herself to dwell upon what Lord Grayden had said to her, or she would find it impossible to keep up her spirits.

They were joined all too soon, she felt, by that gentleman, who was followed by the butler, bearing a huge bouquet of hothouse roses.

"But how divine!" exclaimed Lily, jumping up to admire them. "I wonder who they could be from!"

"They are for Lady Hilary," the butler informed her, bowing.

"Oh? Are they, indeed?" remarked Lily blankly, sinking back into her chair. Never for a moment had she doubted that the flowers would be for her.

Hilary took a brief moment of petty pleasure in her friend's discomfiture. Never before had anyone sent her flowers, while she knew that Lily received cascades of them with regularity.

"Well?" cried Lily, recovering quickly. "Read the card, Hilary! Let's see who your admirer is!"

Hilary opened it and smiled. "They are from Colonel Hague," she replied. "How very kind of him. He says that he hopes to see me at Lady Torrance's ball tonight."

"And so he shall!" Lily exclaimed. "You see how quickly things happen, Hilary? Why, we may have already found you your husband!"

"Perhaps," said Lord Grayden, who had watched this silently, "Lady Hilary feels that she should return to Drake Hall, or that she should write to Mr. Brawley to come to town."

Lily stared at him. "How very odd you are, Grayden," she remarked. "You know very well that I brought Hilary here to escape from that man and his family. I will allow her to do no such thing!"

"I merely thought that Lady Hilary might feel awkward because of her approaching marriage to Mr. Brawley. If she begins to receive the attention of very many gentlemen, especially if she receives the attention of any *one* particular gentleman, we may be making her life more difficult by having her stay."

"Well, what rubbage!" said Lily flatly. "Whatever is making you talk such taradiddle, Grayden? Hilary shall stay right here. There is no formal engagement between them yet, and so if she should decide to marry someone else, there could be no difficulty."

In her heart, Hilary knew what a very decided difficulty there would be with Lord and Lady Werrington, but for the moment she decided not to think of that. Instead, she rang for the butler to bring her some notepaper.

"What are you doing, my dear?" asked Lily anxiously. "You aren't writing to Mr. Brawley, are you?"

"I am not," Hilary replied firmly, looking directly at Grayden. "I am going to write Colonel Hague a note to thank him for the roses and to tell him that I look forward to dancing with him again this evening."

"Bravo!" cried Lily, clapping her hands. "I shall write a letter, too. Mine will be to Mr. Brawley, however. I believe that I shall tell him—" She paused a moment to consider what she should say. "I shall tell him that despite all our efforts you have contracted an infection and that you must avoid the strain of travel for a week or two."

She seated herself beside Hilary and began to write her letter, glancing up thoughtfully at Lord Grayden as she composed it.

"Well, you needn't look at me so forbiddingly, Grayden!" she scolded. "I will not allow Hilary to leave as yet, and I certainly do not wish a horde of Brawleys to descend upon us."

Lord Grayden shrugged, clearly disassociating himself from her activity. After checking his pocket watch, he stood and bowed to them.

"If you will excuse me, ladies, I have an appointment with Gentleman Jackson to go a few rounds with him. I will call for you this evening." He paused a moment on the way out to pat Jack, who considered him a close friend after he had rescued him from Brawley and who demanded his share of attention.

"How very strangely he is acting," mused Lily, looking after him. "It isn't like Grayden to speak so decided an opinion about anything. He always seems quite indifferent to my affairs."

She glanced at Hilary curiously. "He certainly seems to wish to send you away, my dear. Have you done something to offend him?"

"Not that I know of," Hilary replied, feeling a stab of guilt at her disingenuous answer.

She comforted herself with the knowledge that Lily knew that Grayden thought she should return to Drake Hall. There was certainly no need to discuss Lily's role in the matter. Hilary was certain that her friend would not even understand his comment that Hilary was her "toy of the moment" or believe that her behavior might be considered selfish. Hilary had had ample opportunity in her life to observe that selfish people never understand that they are indeed selfish. Lily would be mystified by any criticism of her behavior. And for a brief moment she found herself wondering how Grayden *could* criticize her in such a way and still remain so faithful an admirer.

"Well," Lily sighed, sealing her note a few minutes later. "At least we will be safe from the Brawleys for the time being."

As she prepared for the ball that evening, Hilary noticed that Lucy was unusually quiet. The night before the little maid had fairly bubbled with excitement over being in London and over the beauty of her mistress's gown. She had been quiet upon Hilary's return, but Hilary had ascribed that to the late hour.

Tonight, however, Lucy was equally as silent, even in the face of a second lovely gown. Whatever Lily's shortcomings might be, Hilary thought with satisfaction as Lucy slipped the gown over her head, she could be generous to a fault. She had lavishly supplied her friend with new clothes.

As Lucy fastened her necklace for her, Hilary studied the girl's face in the glass. Her expression was much more solemn than usual, and Hilary was almost certain that she had seen traces of tears earlier in the day. Perhaps a second great change so soon after the first had been too much for Lucy.

Hilary was troubled, but she decided not to mention it just yet. Very possibly the girl would get over her bout of homesickness and be able to enjoy herself in London. It was an opportunity that neither of them was likely to have again for years—if then.

The ball that night was as splendid as the one the night before, and the crowd was just as thick. Happily, Lord Henry did not put in an appearance, and Colonel Hague was gratifyingly attentive, as were the four gallants from the night before. At first Lily tried to keep her close by, as she had the evening before, but as Hilary's admirers appeared and the throng around them grew, she was able to move away.

Lord Grayden remained close by Lily for the duration of the evening, leaving her only briefly to come and offer his services to Hilary should she be in need of refreshments. Seeing her well taken care of, however, he returned to Lily.

That made no difference to Hilary, naturally, for she did not expect him to dance with her. He had not done so the night before when he had told Lord Henry that they were engaged for the next dance, and she had not seen him stand up with Lily during either evening. That was a curious thing, she reflected briefly. He stood close by Lily always, and seemed not to mind when she danced with so many others but never with him.

She did not think about it long, however, for she remained occupied with the tiny court that she had established. On their way home in the carriage, Lily teased her by calling them "Hilary's Army," with Colonel Hague as their commander. Grayden remained silent during her teasing, and Hilary wondered if he were very bored with all of this. In fact, she was so weary that she fell asleep on the way home and had to be awakened when they arrived in Grosvenor Square.

When she entered her chamber, she found neither Jack nor Lucy waiting, as they had been the night before. It was very late, she knew, and Lucy might well have grown weary of waiting for her and gone to bed, but she would not have taken Jack with her to her tiny bedroom in the attic. She started to ring the bell, but decided against it. If Lucy had gone to bed instead of waiting up for her, she was exhausted. The child had shown herself to be very conscientious, so if it were possible for her to be present, she would have been there.

Hilary was at first puzzled about Jack, then worried, and finally decided that she must find him before going to bed. She did not wish to bother Lily with the problem, but she stood in the passageway, uncertain of which direction she should go. It was always possible that if Jack were lonely, he might have managed an escape from the chamber and gone in search of Lucy.

Her difficulty was solved when Jack's sharp, imperative bark sounded faintly through the silence of the house. It came from downstairs, and it was fortunately so muffled that it would probably not arouse anyone not listening for it. Doubtless Jack had gone to sleep unnoticed by anyone and gotten himself closed up in some room downstairs.

Hilary hurried down the steps, holding her candle high to light her way. It was fortunate that the household left some lamps burning during the night so that she could make her way more easily than she would have been able to in pitch-darkness.

When she reached the spacious entrance hall, she paused to listen. She could hear Jack, but the sound was still at a distance. Uncertainly, she swung open a baize door leading to the servants' area and made her way down the backstairs toward the kitchen in the basement.

As she approached the darkened kitchen, she could hear Jack more clearly. He was growling. Hurrying as quickly as she could without tripping over anything, she entered the kitchen and stopped cold. In the corner on the farther side of the hearth was Jack, apparently firmly attached to someone's leg.

"Jack!" she commanded "Come here at once!"

Jack obeyed reluctantly, giving the ankle a final nip as he backed away.

"Damned little beast!" exclaimed the victim. "I'll have him put down! He's ripped my ankle to shreds!"

"Lord Henry!" exclaimed Hilary in horror. "Jack, what have you done?"

She had a sudden vision of this threat being carried out. After all, Jack had attacked the man in his own home. She stared down at her pet.

"Jack, whatever possessed you to do such a thing?" she demanded.

Jack looked at her with speaking eyes and thumped his tail firmly against the brick floor.

"It was for me, miss. Don't let him hurt Jack! The dog wouldn't have bothered him if he hadn't thought I was in trouble."

"Lucy?" asked Hilary in disbelief, as her maid emerged from the dark corner behind Lord Henry. She looked at Lucy's disheveled hair, her cap lying on the floor, the torn bodice of her gown. "What are you doing down here? What has happened?"

"Nothing at all has happened!" snapped Lord Henry, limping past her with a vengeful glance at Jack. "Except that I have been attacked! But you may be certain that something will happen tomorrow morning when I make arrangements to have that little beast taken away and disposed of!"

Jack growled throatily and rose to his feet, causing Lord Henry to increase his speed. The kitchen door swung shut behind him, and Lucy collapsed in tears.

"Tell me what happened, Lucy," Hilary said gently, leading her to the settle beside the hearth.

"Oh, it has been awful, miss, and I am so afraid of him. He bothered me once or twice before, but it was during the daytime when there were others about. I could get away from him then, and no harm done. But tonight—" Here she broke off in a fresh gush of tears.

"What about tonight, Lucy? Tell me about it," Hilary

encouraged her. "How did you come to be down here at such a late hour?"

"Tilly, one of the other maids, came up and told me that you had asked that I have some hot tea ready for you when you got home. So when they left with the carriage to fetch you home, I came down here."

She wiped her eyes. "He must have paid Tilly to do it—or perhaps threatened her—the others say he's that kind of a gentleman."

"A gentleman!" exclaimed Hilary wrathfully. "He is nothing close to being a gentleman!"

"If it hadn't been for Jack," said Lucy, patting his head gratefully, "his plan would have worked just fine. I brought my candle down to work by, and Jack came along, too. I didn't even know Lord Henry was here until he blew out the candle and grabbed me."

She looked at Hilary fearfully. "I'm afraid that I struck him, ma'am. I didn't know who it was, you see, and—"

"You did very well to strike him!" Hilary interrupted her. "It didn't matter whether it was Lord Henry or one of the servants, you had the right to defend yourself. Why did you not scream?"

"He told me that I would be in trouble if I did, and I thought he might be telling the truth. I know some of the other maids have had problems with him, and they haven't said anything. I thought that perhaps things were different here than they are at home."

Hilary swallowed the protests that rose immediately, understanding that what Lucy said was true. With this man in the house, she had left her maid in a most uncomfortable situation without knowing it.

"But you should have told me, Lucy," she replied gently.

"Perhaps so, my lady, but I didn't want to make things difficult for you when you're only here for a few days. I thought that I could stay away from him for that long."

Hilary patted her hand, and Lucy added earnestly, "I did try to struggle, my lady, but then he grabbed both my hands, and I thought that I wasn't going to have a chance until I heard Jack bark. The first thing I knew the gentleman was cursing and shaking his leg and he had to let go of me with one hand in order to try to pry Jack loose."

Hilary regarded her pet with admiration. "Good dog!" she said approvingly. "A very good dog, Jack!" And she set him up on her lap where he settled, comfortably aware that he had done a good night's work.

"Oh, but I'm so sorry, miss, if I've caused you trouble." She looked at Jack, her eyes troubled. "And what if he does try to have Jack destroyed?"

"I should like to see him try any such thing!" retorted Hilary, fire in her eyes. "Lord Henry merely thought that he had a problem tonight. Tomorrow I will make him aware that he truly has one!"

Carrying Jack, she led Lucy back to her own chamber instead of to Lucy's attic room and had the girl sleep on a pallet there for the rest of the night, secure in the knowledge that she was safe from Lord Henry. Early the next morning, when it was safe, Lucy returned to her own room to change and prepare for the day.

Nine

Hilary also rose and prepared for battle. She was not a person given to anger; despite the constant barrage of disparaging remarks from her stepmother during her childhood, she had managed to maintain inner composure as well as outer, rarely allowing such treatment to touch her. She was, however, more vulnerable when the target was not herself. Seldom in her life had she been as furious as she was upon learning of Lord Henry's reprehensible behavior, and she meant to take the matter up with Lily as soon as possible.

When she marched into the drawing room, accompanied by a stiff-legged, vigilant Jack, whom she wasn't leaving alone for a minute for fear Lord Henry would lay hands upon him, she saw that Lord Grayden had already installed himself. He sat at his ease, his long legs, elegantly booted, stretched out before him, and he watched her entrance with interest.

"Whatever is the matter, Hilary?" asked Lily in astonishment, seeing her unusually pink cheeks and her grim expression. "You look excessively angry. Has one of the maids ruined another of your dresses?"

Hilary had regaled her with the story of Marie and the scorching of the terrible mustard gown.

"I'm afraid that it is nothing so inconsequential as a gown, Lily," said Hilary, seating herself close to her friend. "In fact, it is a matter of great importance."

"More important than ruining a gown?" asked Lily lightly. "Then we must be talking about a serious matter indeed."

"It's not to be laughed away, Lily," Hilary replied. And briefly she told her what had befallen Lucy the night before.

"And that episode is what all of this is about?" asked Lily when she had completed her account.

She reached over and patted Hilary's hand. "You have my word, my dear, that nothing will happen to your precious Jack. I know how you dote upon him."

Recognizing his name and a kind tone, Jack wagged his tail approvingly.

"Thank you, Lily. I would naturally not allow Lord Henry to hurt Jack, but I do appreciate your offer of help. What I would like to know, however, is what you intend to do about Lord Henry's behavior."

Lily stared at her. "What do you mean, Hilary? What *should* I do about his behavior? He is merely a man— not a particularly attractive one, I know—but still a man, acting as many men of his rank do."

"Can you mean that you approve of what he did?" demanded Hilary in disbelief. "Are you endorsing his conduct?"

"Well, of course I am not," Lily replied crossly, "but you are making far too much of this. If he had accosted you, I assure you that Lord Carhill and I would have his head on a platter. But you must be realistic, Hilary. Men like Lord Henry frequently take their pleasures with the servants of a house. It is distasteful, but not unusual."

"Well, he will not do so with my maid!" announced Hilary firmly. "I shall have her sleep on a pallet in my room for as long as we are here. And I would appreciate it, Lily," she added, looking into her friend's eyes, "if you would speak to Lord Henry about leaving Lucy alone."

"Speak to him about your maid?" asked Lily, truly astonished now.

Hilary regarded her without blinking. "If you will not, Lily, I shall be forced to disturb Lord Carhill with this business myself, which I should hate to do since he is in such ill health."

"You must not disturb Robert, Hilary," replied Lily quickly. "I will speak to Henry if nothing else will satisfy you, although I daresay that he will not listen to me."

"Nothing else will satisfy me, Lily, and if he does not listen to you—"

Lord Grayden, who had been watching in some amusement, intervened suddenly.

"Are you always so interested in the well-being of your servants, ma'am?" he inquired with a lifted brow.

"Lucy is my responsibility," she replied stiffly. "She is only a child and has never been away from home before. I will not have her abused."

Grayden nodded thoughtfully. Then, studying her coronet of braids a moment, said somewhat irrelevantly, "I am glad that you did not allow Lily's hairdresser to cut your hair."

Annoyed, both by the frivolous change of subject and by his assumption that he had the right to comment upon her appearance, Hilary snapped, "And just what has my hair to say to anything, sir?"

"Merely that the crown of braids suits you," he responded. "I thought so when I first saw you, but I had scarcely had time observe you. Now I would say most definitely that you were correct in keeping it."

"Why?" she demanded irritably. "Because it is old-fashioned?"

She was growing accustomed to his habit of saying

things to throw her off-balance. It was fortunate, she thought briefly, that she had never considered herself a particularly attractive woman, or what self-esteem she possessed would be in shreds.

He shook his head, still regarding her with a judicious eye. "Because it is regal," he replied. "I should imagine that is the way Boudicca wore her hair as she drove out the Romans."

Then he rose, bowed to her briefly, and strolled from the room.

He had succeeded in catching her off-guard again. Hilary had had no time to think of a comment to make in return. Saying that her appearance was regal seemed almost like a tribute, but when he added Boudicca, the matter became less certain. The only sure thing was that, given the comparison, she must look as bloodthirsty as she felt.

"Well, I'm certain that I've never heard Grayden remark on anyone's hair before," said Lily crossly. "I have changed the manner in which I wear mine any number of times without his saying a word."

Since Hilary too thought his observation curious, she could not immediately respond. However, seeing that Lily was offended and wishing her to keep her mind on Lord Henry, she said soothingly, "I daresay he just wished to put me out of countenance."

And she was satisfied that there was truth in the statement. If he had not precisely taken her in dislike, he certainly seemed determined to make her uncomfortable.

"Yes, but why should he wish to do so?" demanded Lily reasonably. "Grayden pays no attention to others. And why should he? He has always done as he pleases. The only person he ever really defers to is Robert."

Hilary was interested in this bit of information. She already knew, of course, that Grayden did as he pleased, but she was surprised to hear that he held Lord Carhill in esteem. That made his relationship with Lily all the more curious.

She reminded herself sharply that her mind was wandering; she must not lose sight of her objective.

"You will not forget to speak to Lord Henry, will you, Lily? You do promise me that?" she said, trying to fix her thoughts on the matter at hand.

"Yes, it is very tiresome and I daresay it will have little effect, Hilary, but I will speak to him." She frowned. "I do wish that Henry would have stayed at the hunting box. I have only been back in London a few weeks, but I knew from the moment we arrived that he would be a thorn to Robert."

"I am sorry to hear that," said Hilary truthfully, hoping to hear more. It did seem unfortunate that a man like Sir Robert would have such a son. "He does not seem to bear any resemblance—either in spirit or body—to his father."

"That is because I am certain that Robert is not his father," replied Lily abruptly.

Hilary stared at her in astonishment. Lily nodded knowingly. "Robert would never tell me that, of course, but I heard as much from several of the ladies we spent time with in Italy and Greece. Robert's older son, Anthony, is the child of his first marriage, and he detests Robert."

"Anthony is Lord Carhill's heir, then?" Hilary asked. Lily's wedding, so many months ago, had been a quiet one, for it had been her husband's third marriage. Hilary had been present, but she did not recall the presence of any of Lord Carhill's family.

Lily nodded. "Anthony does not like me, either," she added. "I have never even met him, but he has not come to London since we returned, and he knows that his father is ill."

"Poor Lord Carhill," sighed Hilary. He had a young wife with a lover, a younger son of whom he could not be proud, and an older one who did not wish to see him.

Lily nodded again. "Robert never speaks of it, though. All that I know I have gathered from other sources. Anthony hated his father for marrying Henry's mother, and I suppose it was a mistake. Lady Westing, whom we met in Rome, confided in me that everyone knew that she took a lover as soon as Lord Carhill married her, and that the lover was Henry's father."

She paused a moment, frowning, then added, "It seems utterly unfair that she would do that to a man like Robert."

Hilary stared at her friend, not only because of the news about Henry but also because Lily appeared to make no connection between the second Lady Carhill and herself. She seemed not to take into account the fact that she was newly married to Lord Carhill herself and that she was seeing Grayden. It was no wonder that Anthony did not wish to come home.

"And what happened to Lord Henry's mother?" asked Hilary curiously. Divorces were virtually unheard of, so she knew the lady must be dead.

"She died of a fever when Henry was just a boy, but Lady Westing said that she had already spoiled Henry so badly that Robert could do little to mend the problem."

"And Henry's father?"

"He fought a duel and killed his man unfairly, apparently. He turned and fired before the count had reached ten, and shot his opponent in the back. The disgrace of it forced him to flee the country," replied Lily. "So you can see that Henry is his son in spirit, and Lady Westing said that he is very like him in face and figure."

"Yet Lord Carhill has always treated him as his son?"

"Naturally," Lily said. "Robert does his best for him. Henry sent countless letters to him while we were abroad, all of them asking for more money or for help with some scrape or another. I knew what to expect of him before I ever laid eyes upon him."

Hilary sighed. Life had been decidedly unfair to Lord Carhill, who appeared to her to deserve a much better hand than he had been dealt.

Lily did as she had promised and spoke with Henry about his attack upon Lucy. However, fearful that Lily had been correct and that Lord Henry would not listen to her, Hilary decided that she must take measures of her own without bothering Lord Carhill.

In order to protect Lucy as much as possible, Jack was left in Lucy's company whenever Hilary was gone. This had helped Lucy's and Hilary's peace of mind, but it had done little for some other members of the household. One of Jack's first acts as protector had been to bite one of the footmen when he was too free with unwanted attentions to Lucy. That, coupled with the rumored attack upon Lord Henry, persuaded the male members of the household to give Lucy and Jack as wide a berth as possible.

Although she felt more secure about Lucy, Hilary's peace of mind was badly cut up in another respect. Despite the fact that she was certain that Lord Grayden felt no admiration for her, he seemed determined to single her out. It was not at all surprising that he was always with them, because Hilary was almost always with Lily. However, after the episode of Lucy and Lord Henry, he appeared more interested in her and frequently turned the conversation her way.

At Lady Ballinger's ball, he singled her out and led her to a small table screened by a group of potted palms.

"Tell me, Lady Hilary," he murmured, drawing his chair closer to hers. "Has Lord Henry been keeping well away from your maid? Or have you been compelled to set Jack upon him once again?"

"He has kept his distance, my lord," she replied stiffly. "I appreciate your interest, however."

"You must know that I am always interested in your welfare, ma'am," he responded, taking her hand. "Lord Henry has not troubled you, has he?"

Hilary's eyes flashed. "I should dearly like to see him try to do so!" she replied, and she deftly withdrew her hand from his.

Lord Grayden laughed. "I should like to see that myself," he agreed. "I almost pity Henry."

Hilary regarded him with dismay. She knew that she amused and interested him—rather like a child with a new toy, she had thought, smiling to herself ironically. How very peculiar that he should accuse Lily of the same thing that he was guilty of himself. He clearly regarded her as an amusement, a new way to pass the time.

"I assure you that Lord Henry is in need of no pity," she replied. "And, as long as he does not trouble Lucy or Jack, he will not be troubled by me."

"I believe he knows that," Lord Grayden agreed. "I had a talk with him today, and he appeared to understand that rather well."

"Did you indeed?" she asked, startled. "How kind of you to do so, Lord Grayden. I am most grateful."

He bowed briefly. "Not at all. I feared that you would make short work of Lord Henry, and his humiliation and your unhappiness would grieve Lord Carhill."

"Yes, I am certain that it would," she agreed, still

staring at him. How very odd that he should care so much for Lord Carhill's equanimity when he himself danced attendance upon Lady Carhill. It was all a little more than she could take in, and she decided that she must be very countrified in her outlook.

She thought for a moment that Lord Grayden was going to forget himself so far as to ask her to dance with him, but he caught himself in time and bowed.

"I regret that I must leave you and Lady Carhill," he said, bending over her hand and staring into her eyes for a breathless moment. "I have had a message from a friend of mine just an hour ago, and he has asked that I meet him at our club. I have not seen the gentleman in several years and his business seems pressing; otherwise, I assure you that I would not leave you. I have arranged for the carriage to be brought round in half an hour and Colonel Hague has agreed to escort you and Lily out."

He departed, leaving her to her other admirers for the last bit of the evening. She was certain that he felt no real attraction to her, but she was very puzzled by his attentiveness.

Unfortunately, Hilary was not the only one to notice his attentions. On their way home from the ball that night, Lily said, "I am amazed that Grayden is not seeing us home instead of rushing off to his club to see that friend of his. He always escorts me home, and now that he seems to be dancing attendance upon you, I thought we would be sure of his company."

"Well, it is natural to want to see him," said Hilary soothingly, for Lily's feathers were clearly ruffled. "I understand that Lord Grayden has not seen the gentleman for several years."

"How very interesting that you should know that, Hilary," Lily responded, a decided edge in her tone.

"What do you mean, Lily?"

"I mean that you know that he has not seen the man for several years, while I do not. Grayden did not see fit to mention that to me."

"He must have told me that while Mr. Gregory was dancing with you," said Hilary consolingly. "There is no question that you above anyone should know his plans."

"That is exactly what I feel," sniffed Lily, "but it is not what is happening. Grayden appears to be actually *talking* to you; he merely makes conversation with me."

Hilary had the uncomfortable feeling that this was true, and she wished that Lily had not chosen this particular moment to grow perceptive about others.

"I do not see how I am to make a successful marriage for you in such a short time if Grayden behaves like this," continued Lily fretfully. "Why, even Colonel Hague had difficulty winning your attention tonight, for Grayden was so often speaking with you. I shall take up the matter with him tomorrow. I would almost think he is deliberately trying to interfere with your chance to find someone to replace Mr. Brawley."

She looked at Hilary as though to measure the effect of her words.

"I cannot think why he would wish to do that," responded Hilary uneasily. "He has no reason to protect Mr. Brawley's interests."

"Not unless he feels that what we are doing is not honorable," said Lily slowly, "for, even though he appears so indifferent about everything, he does have his own code of honor. Or unless," and here she eyed Hilary speculatively, "unless he has a reason of his own for spoiling your chances."

"Perhaps he merely has a heartless nature," observed Hilary offhandedly, wishing to drop the subject, "and wishes to see me firmly ensconced at Drake Hall."

Lily shrugged, and they lapsed into silence. What bothered Hilary more than Lily's comments was a realization that she had made just tonight: she enjoyed talking with Grayden. Even if he disapproved of her—or of her action in coming to London—he addressed her as though she were an intelligent human being, and he was interesting. He was unsettling, very unsettling, but interesting.

She could not allow herself to think that she felt drawn to him. That was a thought that had arisen briefly tonight as he looked down into her eyes, laughing at something she had said, and she had caught a glimpse of something that looked suspiciously like tenderness. She had been wrong, of course, but she had felt an answering warmth in her own glance.

She sighed, knowing how foolish it was to indulge herself in such a fancy. Firmly she put it from her mind, seeking to place it in a locked compartment as she had her thoughts about the Brawleys, and forced herself to think of other things.

As she climbed the stairs to her chamber and said good night to Lily, she resolutely turned her thoughts to how grateful she must be to return to a warm greeting from Jack and Lucy. That might not be much, she thought sadly, but it was more than Lord Carhill had.

She did not go directly to sleep that night but sat long beside her fire, sketchbook in hand, using it as she always had: to make light of her experiences and to escape from realities she did not wish to acknowledge. Lord Henry appeared, the picture of virtue outraged, with Jack firmly attached to his ankle and a hapless feminine victim huddled in the background, and Hilary promptly titled it "Virtue Saved by a Canine Paladin."

She could not think of any light way to treat the matter of Lord Carhill and Lily, however. She puzzled over it for a moment, then turned to the back of her book and began a series of different sketches—her "what-if" series—in which she pictured things the way she wished they were.

The first thing she captured was Lily seated on the arm of Lord Carhill's chair, leaning on his shoulder and smiling at him affectionately. That much had been real and served as the inspiration for the rest. Her next one was of Lily and Lord Carhill strolling down Bond Street, Lily's arm tucked through his as she looked up at him in the same manner she looked at Grayden.

She worked rapidly for over an hour and then studied her set with satisfaction. That was the way she wished their life could be, and she felt a certain satisfaction that she had managed at least that much happiness for Lord Carhill—even if it were only on paper.

Ten

Lord Carhill was still on her mind when she awoke the next morning. Remembering she had promised him that she would stop in to see him, she asked Lily hesitantly if he might be feeling well enough to receive a visitor.

"You wish to see Robert?" she asked in some surprise, pausing in the scolding she had been administering to Lord Grayden for not seeing them home from the ball last night.

"Yes, I would very much like to speak with him," answered Hilary, ignoring Grayden's interested expression.

"You don't mean to tell him about Henry, do you?" Lily inquired apprehensively. "For I must warn you, Hilary—"

"No, nothing more has happened, Lily, and I certainly don't wish to distress Lord Carhill. But he did ask me to come in and see him, and I haven't done so since the night we arrived."

"Oh, he said that just to be polite, Hilary. You need not feel obligated to do so." Lily dismissed the idea with a wave of her hand.

"I don't feel obligated, Lily," Hilary assured her, "and I don't wish to intrude if he doesn't want callers, but I thought that he might be lonely."

Lily stared at her for a moment. "Lonely? Robert?"

The novelty of the notion appeared to take her aback. "Nonsense! Robert is never lonely. He has his books and the occasional caller—and of course I go in to see him every morning and before I leave in the evening. How should he be lonely?"

"How many callers has he had since we have returned?" asked Lord Grayden. "Aside from the three of us?"

Lily thought it over, her dimpled face serious. "Well, I know Mr. Hastings has been here, and I believe perhaps Lord Winchell called, too."

"So he has had one—or, at the most two—callers? And undoubtedly they remained only briefly in order not to tire him?" returned Grayden, glancing at Hilary.

Lily nodded. "So you see, he could not be lonely. If anything, he probably wishes for more rest."

"You know how active he was before his illness, Lily, and there is certainly nothing amiss with his mind. How can you say he would wish just for more rest?" demanded Lord Grayden. "Would you be happy if being confined to that chamber were your lot instead of his?"

"No, of course not!" she replied indignantly. "But that would be quite a different matter, Grayden, because I am young and—"

"I don't think it is such a different matter," he interrupted. "You wish for it to be a different matter, but that does not make it so. Lady Hilary is correct. She should go up to see him if he is feeling well enough for callers."

Lily arose and pulled the bell cord for the butler, her manner huffy. "But of course Lady Hilary is correct," she said acidly. "She has only met Robert once and I am his wife, but she undoubtedly knows more than I do about his situation."

"Lily, I've no wish to upset you—" began Hilary, but Lord Grayden once more interrupted.

"Never mind upsetting Lily," he responded. "Your instincts were quite correct. Going to see Lord Carhill is more important than catering to Lily's whims."

"Catering to my whims?" gasped Lily indignantly. "Grayden, you really do take too much upon yourself! Robert would be most displeased if he were to hear you say that to me!"

"And do you plan to tell him?" inquired Grayden pleasantly. "I believe that you just warned Lady Hilary against upsetting him with any unpleasant news."

He watched her expression with interest. "Ah, it is quite a struggle, isn't it, Lily? Which to give way to, your pride or your self-interest? That is a difficult choice."

"I would never upset Robert," Lily replied coolly, attempting to regain her dignity. "If you think that I would, then I see that you don't know me as well as you think, Grayden."

"I know you like the back of my hand, Lily," he assured her, "so don't try to play the great lady with me."

Fortunately the butler entered before she was forced to respond, and she turned to him haughtily, telling him to inquire of Lord Carhill's valet whether he could receive a visitor, for Lady Hilary wished to call upon him.

As the butler bowed and made his exit, Lily turned and said coldly, "And now, if you will excuse me, I must go upstairs to prepare for the gathering at Lady Sefton's. Do you plan to attend with me, Hilary, or will you spend the entire afternoon ministering to Lord Carhill?"

"Naturally I will go with you, Lily," responded Hilary. "Pray don't be angry with me."

"Oh, I am not angry with you," she replied in a distant tone. "I do think, however, that there are some people who sadly underestimate me."

And with that she swept from the room.

"I am sorry that I set her off," sighed Hilary, "but I had been thinking of Lord Carhill and I do wish to see him."

"May I ask why you had been thinking of Carhill?" asked Lord Grayden curiously.

Hilary flushed and did not meet his eyes. She could scarcely tell him that part of the reason was that she felt life had been so unfair to the man. Since he was part of that unfairness, being Lily's lover, that would scarcely be possible. Instead, she told him part of the truth.

"I enjoyed his company on that first night," she responded. "He is a very intelligent, kindly man."

"Indeed he is," agreed Grayden. "However, I think there is more to it than that, since you awakened this morning with Lord Carhill on your mind when you did not for the past few days. Why today?"

Hilary shook her head again, still avoiding his eyes. "I'm sure I couldn't say, Lord Grayden," she responded. "Who is to say why some thoughts enter our minds at particular times?"

"True enough," he conceded, "and I can see that you think that I'm hounding you. But in truth, Lady Hilary, I find the workings of your mind quite fascinating."

"Do you indeed?" she asked, bristling. "And what makes you think that you know the workings of my mind, sir?"

"But that's precisely it," he said. "I don't know them. On the other hand, I know precisely how Lady Carhill's mind works. Hers is not difficult at all."

"And so that is what I represent to you—a puzzle?" Hilary replied.

"Unlike Lily, you underestimate yourself, Lady Hilary," he returned smoothly, suddenly putting out his hand to smooth a curl that had escaped from its proper place. The warmth and gentleness of his touch made her heart give an unexpected lurch, but she did not betray it by even the flicker of an eyelash.

"Do I indeed?" she asked politely, forcing herself to meet his eyes coolly.

"Yes indeed," he returned, smiling slowly. The glimpse of tenderness that she had caught in his eyes the night before had returned and she felt it almost impossible to look away from him. It was no wonder that Lily wished him above all others to be her cicisbeo. A cynic he well might be, but a fascinating one.

Leaning closer, he cupped his hand around her cheek and kissed her lips gently. "I wish that you might spare me just a portion of the concern you show for Lord Carhill," he said in a low voice. "Have you none to spare for me, ma'am?"

"Pardon me, Lady Hilary," announced the butler from the doorway, "but Lord Carhill will see you now."

Gratefully Hilary rose and made her escape. She was not certain what game Grayden was playing, but that he *was* playing one she was certain. She could not allow herself to be taken in. He had no real interest in her beyond her amusement value, she was certain, and she had no wish to play at cat-and-mouse with him. She was all too certain who the mouse was. Nor would she allow herself to dwell upon how pleasant she found such attentions.

It was a relief to step once more into the comfortable safety of Lord Carhill's chamber. And she realized with a sudden shock of recognition that safety was the feeling she connected with him and with this room—a very curious reaction to have after just one meeting. The only other person with whom she had ever felt safe was Clara—and even then there had been an element of uneasiness, for Clara herself had no power and the safety could disappear at the whim of Lord or Lady Werrington.

With Lord Carhill, however, she felt a rocklike safety, even though he was ill. It was, she thought, because he was both a powerful man and a trustworthy one; although how she had known at first meeting that he was trustworthy, she could not say. Now, of course, she had seen his treatment of Lily and Henry. She had solid evidence that, at least where his family was concerned, he was a man to be trusted. Again she found herself envying Lily, whose rock he was.

Ignoring her protest, Lord Carhill rose from his chair as she entered to bow to her and take her hand.

"I am delighted that you have made time to come to see me, Lady Hilary," he said, smiling.

"You must not stand up on my account," she said. "Pray do not tire yourself, Lord Carhill, or I'll know I should not have bothered you."

"Then I shall sit down immediately," he assured her, "for I do wish to have you return. I will have you know, however," he added in a tone of great pride, "that Walton and I have walked back and forth across this room three times this morning."

Walton, his devoted valet, hovered protectively in the background. He nodded his affirmation of Lord Carhill's statement, bowing to Hilary.

"I am delighted to hear that, sir," Hilary replied, smiling. "If you have done so much, though, perhaps it would be best if I came in later. You must need to rest after such exertion."

"Nonsense!" he exclaimed, in what was almost a robust voice. "Walton will bring us some refreshments, and I shall have the pleasure of your company. *Then* I may be persuaded to nap."

Taking his cue, Walton bowed again and left in search of the requested refreshments.

"And what of you, Lady Hilary?" he asked. "Have you been enjoying your stay?"

"Oh, indeed I have," she replied sincerely. "I cannot think of anything I would have preferred to do than to come with Lily for these few days. You have both been very kind to me."

He bowed to her. "I only wish that I were able to be a proper host for you, my dear, but I'm afraid that is impossible for the moment."

"You appear to be gaining strength, sir, so perhaps it will not be long now before you will be able to do your walking outside this chamber." And she thought suddenly of her sketch of him strolling happily down Bond Street with Lily.

He nodded. "That is my hope. If you will but remain with us long enough—which is also my hope, by the way—I may very well do precisely that. I may even be able to escort you both to the theater."

"I know that you will soon be able to do so, Lord Carhill," she said, feeling more hopeful about his health than she had after her first call. His face had more color and his eyes were brighter—altogether he looked much better than he had. "I am afraid, though, that I shall be leaving before very much longer."

"Indeed?" he asked, looking disappointed. "We had hoped that you would spend some time with us, my dear, quite as long as you would like, in fact."

He paused a moment as though considering his next words carefully, and added, "I hope that I do not offend you, Lady Hilary, but my wife gave me to understand that your situation is not a particularly happy one."

Hilary appreciated his delicacy, but she still flushed

as she met his eyes. "That is regrettably true, Lord Carhill, but I do not wish to complain. Many women do not make a marriage of their choice, so I am not alone in that."

As soon as the words had crossed her lips, she wished them back. She had been thinking of herself and not at all of him and the young wife he had taken. It was true that Lily had chosen him, but Hilary also knew the reasons for her choice. She could not think of what to say to soften it, so she went on, for the moment not meeting his eyes.

"I will be well provided for," she continued, "but there is no one in the household, including Mr. Brawley himself, with whom I am able to talk. That sounds a minor thing, I should imagine, but—"

"It does not sound at all a minor thing," he assured her. "I know from personal experience that having no one to talk to in a marriage, let alone in a whole household, can be unspeakably miserable—even for the man, who has by far the greater advantage in terms of having other relationships."

Her eyes flew to his face, but he was smiling. "No, I do not refer to my relationship with the present Lady Carhill," he responded gently. "However, I have not always been so fortunate in my choice of wife."

Somewhat astonished by his assessment of Lily as a wife, Hilary managed a smile.

"There, that is much better, my dear," he said. "You need not fear that you will hurt me. I know that I am a much older man than my wife, but she was precisely the proper choice for me: She is lively and amusing and very attentive to me. Some have married younger women only to have them run away with the best silver and the most handsome footman. So, you see, I am quite lucky."

His tone was sincere and not mocking, and his expression seemed content. Perhaps she had imagined the shadow that had crossed his face on the first evening. Or, perhaps he was doing what she had done all her life: making the best of a difficult situation. Lily might not have run off with the footman and the silver, but she was undoubtedly entangled with Grayden, something that an intelligent man like Lord Carhill would certainly know.

Walton returned with a tray, and as they ate they made light conversation about Madame Vestris and about their favorite poems by Sir Walter Scott. It was clear to Hilary that Lord Carhill was rapidly growing weary, however; and when she caught Walton's eye, he nodded.

When Hilary stood to take her leave, Lord Carhill took her hand once more, and aroused himself enough to speak to her, though his voice was low.

"Remember what I said, Lady Hilary. You may stay with us as long as you wish, and you may come to us at any time you wish to do so. Thank you for coming to see an old man, my dear."

She murmured thank you as he squeezed her hand, and then returned thoughtfully to her chamber to prepare for the card party at Lady Sefton's. She managed to push the thought of Lord Grayden's kiss from her mind and to concentrate upon her predicament with the Brawleys.

What if she decided not to marry Mr. Brawley? she wondered. Just what would happen? Unquestionably, her father would be excessively angry, perhaps angry enough to refuse to allow her to live with him any longer. Could she become a governess like Clara? Could she and Clara find teaching positions at some school? She certainly did not wish to do either, even if it were possible. Would Colonel Hague, as Lily suggested, perhaps wish to marry her? Even if he did, he would assuredly not want to assume the burden of her family, so her father would not permit the marriage.

Perhaps, she thought, she should not return to the Brawleys, but if she did not, she had no idea what she would do. Lord Carhill might regret his generous invitation, she reflected grimly. He could find himself with a permanent hanger-on established in his household.

And she found herself wondering just what Lord Grayden would think of that.

Eleven

Lily had recovered her equanimity by the time they departed for Lady Sefton's and appeared to be in great good humor during the course of the afternoon. Being not particularly fond of cards and only a passable player, Hilary contented herself with watching the others and conversing with one or two of the ladies who chose not to play. One of them, a stout matron swathed in pink silk, appeared to take a particular liking to her.

"You do remind me of my eldest daughter, Emma," Lady Gray reflected. "She was always my favorite."

"Then I take that as a compliment," said Hilary, smiling.

Her companion nodded complacently. "Tall and slender, Emma was," she said. "Just the opposite of me."

"Was?" asked Hilary tentatively, fearful that the lady was about to embark upon a family tragedy, although she did not look in the least tragic.

Lady Gray nodded again, selecting another pastry from the tray carried by a passing footman. "Now she looks just like me, only taller," she remarked, laughing. "Four children can take their toll upon one."

"So I should imagine," agreed Hilary, startled, but relieved that Emma was still among the living. "Have you other grandchildren?" she asked politely.

"I have ten," responded the matron proudly. "The

oldest is twenty-five and the youngest is five. Handsome children, all of them."

"I'm certain they are," replied Hilary. "They must give you great pleasure."

"They do indeed," answered Lady Gray, her cheerful countenance suddenly clouding as she glanced over at Lily. "I've always thought it a great shame that Carhill's elder son is estranged from him. Otherwise, Carhill would have the joy of knowing his own grandchildren."

Hilary was surprised by this unexpected reference to Lord Carhill, but very interested, so she remained silent, hoping to learn more.

Lady Gray finished the last bite of her pastry and continued, "As it is, perhaps he will soon have a new child of his own, and that would give him the happiness he deserves."

Startled, Hilary stared at her, uncertain of just what to say. Lady Gray's comment had taken her completely off-guard. As far as she knew, Lily had no thought of having children—or, if she did, no thought of having Carhill's children.

"I'm not simply an old gossip," Lady Gray continued cheerfully, interpreting Hilary's reaction correctly, "although I *am* an old gossip, of course. Carhill and I were youngsters together, and he was a wonderful boy. Everyone loved him."

"I can well believe it," replied Hilary warmly.

Lady Gray looked at her approvingly. "I see that you feel just as you should. It is unfortunate that not everyone sees his value." Her gaze darkened once more as she looked again at Lily.

"If you have influence with your friend, Lady Hilary, perhaps you can do them both some good," she added. "Carhill deserves more from life than he has gotten."

"Lady Carhill is very fond of her husband," said

Hilary tentatively, knowing that in this, at least, she spoke the truth.

Lady Gray snorted inelegantly. "I've heard from a friend of mine in Rome that the gigolos were thick around her, and that she encouraged them all. And I've seen with my own eyes how she is here—like a butterfly in the midst of a field of flowers. And I would have thought better of Grayden than to dance attendance upon her, too."

Hilary longed to hear more on that particular subject, but they were joined just then by two other women, and the conversation turned to more general topics. As the others drifted away, with Lady Gray asking that she call upon her soon, Hilary was left thinking about what the matron had said. Upon one point, they were in complete agreement. So kind a man as Lord Carhill had surely been shortchanged by life.

She glanced at Lily, who was playing cards as she did everything else—in a highly animated style, entertaining the rest of the table with some tale from her travels. She never had a problem taking center stage, whether she knew her audience or not.

Helping Lord Carhill with Lily seemed to be a complete impossibility. She was Lily's friend, to be sure, but she was the recipient of help at the present moment, not the dispenser of it. And Lily certainly felt that she needed no help, least of all from Hilary. Hilary was less certain about Lord Carhill's state of mind.

By the time they left Lady Sefton's, she was no closer to an idea of how she could improve Lord Carhill's lot than she had been. Pottering about in her sketchbook was as close as she could come to taking action, and that did him no good.

She sighed. She could not even help herself, so how in heaven's name could she help Lord Carhill?

"You are very serious," observed Lily during the carriage ride home. "Being too serious is not a helpful quality, Hilary. Most men are very frightened by it."

"Hmm," responded Hilary, still puzzling over her insoluble problems.

"You see?" exclaimed Lily, aggravated. "What man is going to tolerate having a woman say 'Hmm' to something he has just said? You must be more attentive, Hilary, more lively!"

"I beg your pardon, Lily," Hilary said, suddenly focused on Lily's vivid little face, which she had placed directly in front of Hilary's so that she could make eye contact.

"You see! That is exactly what I mean!" said Lily in exasperation. "You are just now hearing what I was saying to you. If I were a man, dear Hilary, I would be well on my way to a woman who would gaze longingly into my eyes and hang upon my every word."

"Well, if you were a man, you would be welcome to do precisely that," retorted Hilary. "As it is, since you are my friend, I apologize for not listening to what you were saying."

"And I accept your apology, but that is not what I want! I want you to see what you need to do in order to attach an eligible gentleman so that you will not have to return to the House of Brawleys!" said Lily. "I know that you want that no more than I do, but you won't listen to my advice, Hilary, and we have so little time!"

Recognizing Lily's sincerity, Hilary apologized again. And she sighed, which was an error in judgment, for Lily again went into action.

"You see? If you sit about and sigh all the time, who will ever decide that you are the woman that he needs, Hilary?" she demanded. "Do you not know that a man wishes to do the sighing and to have the woman ask him what is wrong so that she may make it right? You are so very intelligent, Hilary. How is it that you don't know that?"

Hilary felt very much as though Jack had just set upon her. Lily, she decided, had some very terrier-like characteristics: Once she had a notion, she worried it to death, attacking it from every angle possible with the sharpest of small white teeth. The comparison cheered her and, without thinking, she smiled.

"Yes, Hilary! That is what you must do! Smile, even if you do not feel like it. Smile! That is what gentlemen like!"

"Do they indeed?" replied Hilary, mystified. "Are you trying to tell me, Lily, that if I go about smiling and asking gentlemen what is troubling them when they appear despondent, they will like me?"

"I assure you it is so," responded Lily emphatically. "I have proven it again and again. And of course, when they have done something—even if it is something that does not particularly impress you—you must admire them inordinately. If we are to find you a husband, you must learn to do these things."

"I see," responded Hilary, puzzling over this for a moment.

Suddenly she remembered Lord Carhill talking about Lily and about why he was so fortunate to have her as his wife. What had he said? She concentrated for a moment and the words came back to her: *She is lively and amusing and very attentive to me.*

She looked at her friend with a new respect: Lily was exactly right. If even Lord Carhill felt that way, surely lesser men did as well.

"What are you thinking, Hilary?" demanded Lily, who had been watching her carefully.

"I am thinking, Lily, that you know exactly what you are talking about. I shall take your advice to heart."

Greatly cheered by this breakthrough, Lily hugged

her impulsively, setting Hilary's new bonnet with its bright sprig of cherries wildly askew over one ear.

"We shall find you a husband yet!" she exclaimed triumphantly.

Hilary was less certain of that, but she did feel that she had been granted fresh insight into the relationships between women and men. And she decided that she would put it to the test that very evening. If she could attract Lord Grayden's attention, she might be able to divert him from Lily so that she would consider Lord Carhill more seriously and give him more of her attention. Of course, she admitted to herself, she did not think that she would mind being the object of Grayden's attentions, at least for a little while—and even if that meant accepting a kiss or two.

Accordingly, when Lord Grayden called for the two ladies to escort them to the three routs they planned to attend that night, he found a somewhat different Hilary.

The difference was not immediately apparent to him, but, as the evening wore on, it came forcefully to his attention. Hilary and Lily had both danced the first two dances while Grayden looked on as he normally did, his arms folded. Colonel Hague returned Hilary to her place and remained chatting a moment after engaging her for a quadrille. After he had left, Hilary turned to Grayden.

"Are you quite all right, Lord Grayden?" she asked, her voice low and her tone serious.

He looked at her, mildly startled. "Yes, of course I am all right, Lady Hilary. What causes you to ask?"

"Merely that I saw you standing here while we were dancing, and I was afraid—" She broke off, blushing prettily.

"You were afraid of what?" he asked, more puzzled still.

"I was afraid that you were lonely," she replied, her

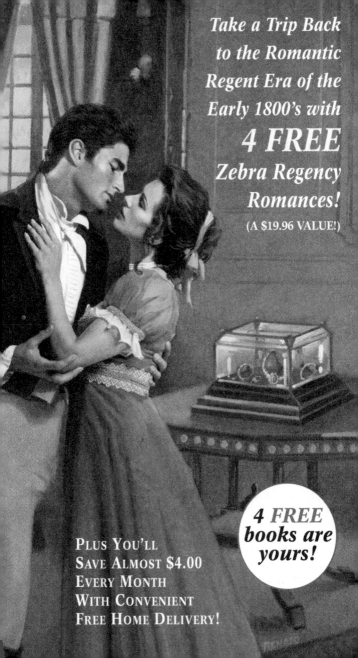

We'd Like to Invite You to Subscribe to Zebra's Regency Romance Book Club and Give You a Gift of 4 Free Books as Your Introduction! (Worth $19.96!)

If you're a Regency lover, imagine the joy of getting **4 FREE Zebra Regency Romances** and then the chance to have the lovely stories delivered to your home each month at the lowest price available! Well, that's our offer to you and here how you benefit by becoming a Regency Romance subscriber:

- **4 FREE** Introductory Regency Romances are delivered to your doorst
- **4 BRAND NEW** Regencies are then delivered each month (usually befor they're available in bookstores)
- Subscribers save almost $4.00 every month
- Home delivery is always **FREE**
- You also receive a **FREE** monthly newsletter, which features author profiles, discounts, subscriber benefits, book previews and more
- No risks or obligations...in other words, you can cancel whenever yo wish with no questions asked

Join the thousands of readers who enjoy the savings and convenience offered to Regency Romance subscribers. After your initial introductory shipment, you receive 4 brand-new Zebra Regency Romances each month to examine for 10 days. Then, if you decide to keep the books, you'll pay the preferred subscriber's price of just $4.00 per title. That's only $16.00 for all 4 books and there's never an extra charge for shipping and handling.

It's a no-lose proposition, so return the FREE BOOK CERTIFICATE today!

Say Yes to 4 Free Books!
Complete and return the order card to receive this $19.96 value, ABSOLUTELY FREE!

If the certificate is missing below, write to:
Regency Romance Book Club
P.O. Box 5214, Clifton, New Jersey 07015-5214
or call TOLL-FREE 1-888-345-BOOK
Visit our website at www.kensingtonbooks.com.

FREE BOOK CERTIFICATE

YES! Please rush me 4 Zebra Regency Romances without cost or obligation. I understand that each month thereafter I will be able to preview 4 brand-new Regency Romances FREE for 10 days. Then, if I should decide to keep them, I will pay the money-saving preferred subscriber's price of just $16.00 for all 4...that's a savings of almost $4 off the publisher's price with no additional charge for shipping and handling. I may return any shipment within 10 days and owe nothing, and I may cancel this subscription at any time. My 4 FREE books will be mine to keep in any case.

Name _____

Address _____ Apt. _____

City_____ State_____ Zip_____

Telephone (   ) _____

Signature _____
(If under 18, parent or guardian must sign.)

RN091A

Terms and prices subject to change. Orders subject to acceptance by Regency Romance Book Club.
Offer valid in U.S. only.

||...||...||...||.||.||.||.||.||.||.||.||.||.||.||...|

REGENCY ROMANCE BOOK CLUB
Zebra Home Subscription Service, Inc.
P.O. Box 5214
Clifton NJ 07015-5214

voice still low and intimate. "Perhaps it would be better were you to ask a lady to dance."

Grayden shook his head emphatically. "I have no desire to dance, Lady Hilary—not with anyone."

Hilary placed her hand on his arm and looked up into his dark eyes. "I am sorry, Lord Grayden. Have I hurt you by bringing it up? You appear so unhappy."

"I was not before you began speaking," replied Grayden grimly, "but I am beginning to feel that I may well be very unhappy, Lady Hilary. What are you playing at?"

Hilary looked at him indignantly, rapidly shedding her sympathetic role. "I am not playing at anything, Lord Grayden!" she replied crisply. "I was merely trying to show you that I felt the pain that you must be feeling as you watched Lady Carhill dance."

"And why should I be feeling any pain over that?" he asked, feeling that he had stumbled into a quagmire. "Lily dances well enough, so why should watching her be painful?"

"Why, because of your great attachment to her, of course! It must trouble you to see so many men pursuing her!" responded Hilary, aggravation overcoming her resolution to try Lily's technique. "I had not thought you so beef-witted!"

He executed a brief bow. "Forgive me, ma'am. I had no notion that I was being beef-witted." He looked at her for a moment. "And could you explain to me, Lady Hilary, just what you think you are doing?"

"I will do no such thing!" she exclaimed. "I believe that I have done my best, but you, sir, are quite impossible!" And Hilary sailed away, head held high, leaving Lord Grayden completely mystified.

Hilary sighed. Her first attempt at carrying out Lily's instructions had been an unqualified failure. She had thought that if she could attach Grayden, even temporarily, that Lord Carhill and Lily might have a little better time of it, but obviously that was not going to work.

In the distance she saw Colonel Hague and smiled as he looked up. To her pleasure, he started to make his way across the room to her. She would practice Lily's magic upon him.

By the end of the evening, Hilary had no notion whether she had made any headway at all. Every time she had looked up during the course of the evening, Grayden had been watching her with lifted brows, as though he was expecting her to do something else peculiar.

As for Lily's method, Hilary had been able to practice only upon the colonel and the rest of her "army," so that could not be considered a fair test. They were already quite taken with her. The only thing she had accomplished with certainty was exhausting herself. Clearly, she did not have the fortitude to be either an actress or a flirt.

She was quiet in the carriage on the way home, while Lily chattered and clung to Grayden's arm, recounting various victories and jokes of the evening.

When she paused for breath, he said, "And what of your evening, Lady Hilary? I hope that everyone was not as beef-witted this evening as I."

"That would scarcely have been possible," returned Hilary shortly.

"Beef-witted? What are you talking about? What happened?" asked Lily.

"I believe that I disappointed Lady Hilary," he replied gravely, watching Hilary's face.

"How could you have disappointed her?" Lily demanded, determined to get to the bottom of the matter.

"I would not dance," said Grayden.

Lily laughed and patted Hilary on the knee. "Grayden never dances, Hilary dear. It is a point of honor with him. It is a great triumph for me that he mingles with us lesser mortals at all."

"Indeed?" remarked Hilary. "His behavior seems remarkably strange to me—but then, of course, it really doesn't matter to me whether he does or does not dance."

"But I thought that Grayden just said—"

"Lord Grayden said what he believes to be true," she said shortly, turning toward the window. "I cannot help it if he is wrong. Could we talk about something else, please?"

Lily stared at her and then at Lord Grayden. "This is all most peculiar," she complained. "I don't understand a bit of it."

"Then you are not alone, Lily," Grayden assured her, studying Hilary's face as the carriage passed through a patch of lamplight.

When she went to bed that night, Hilary promised herself that she would not try Lily's technique again. She could not help Lord Carhill by making a conquest of Grayden. She would be herself and if that was not sufficient, then it was just unfortunate. They were never going to find her a husband in so short a time anyway, and she certainly had no wish to marry someone for whom she would always have to smile and provide comfort and wear a mask. In fact, at the moment she felt in significant need of comfort herself.

As though he could read her thoughts, Jack suddenly hopped up on her bed and curled up against her, laying his head across her knees.

"I tried to help Lord Carhill, Jack," she said solemnly. She frequently chatted with the dog, finding that it helped her sort out her thoughts. "I really did do my best, but I could no more attach Lord Grayden than I could become the Queen of England. Undoubtedly, he has already forgotten that he kissed me. I could as easily have been Lucy so far as he is concerned."

Caught by her tone, Jack raised his head and regarded her seriously.

"And so, Jack, I cannot help Lord Carhill, I cannot help Lily, and I cannot help us. Altogether, I have failed."

Jack fell across her knees again, providing what consolation he could with his warm, furry presence.

"You are a comfort, Jack," she told him, stroking his head. In the stillness, she could hear the reassuring thump of his tail against the counterpane.

"And we know it wouldn't have worked anyway," she whispered, as though someone other than Jack might hear her. "Just think about it. How could a man infatuated by Lily fall in love with me?"

Jack appeared to have no answer to this, and soon she could hear his faint, even snoring. She sighed. She did not even have Jack to talk to now.

She closed her eyes and tried to shut out the Brawleys, but they kept creeping from their compartment into the rest of her mind. As she slipped into sleep, she saw herself being married but, try as she might, she could not see the face of the groom.

Twelve

The next morning she decided that not being able to see the face of the groom had probably been a blessing. Had she seen Mr. Brawley's face as she was just drifting into sleep, the night would doubtless have been punctuated with nightmares. As it was, she had slept dreamlessly, and she and Jack awakened only as Lucy opened the curtains and brought in her tea.

The little maid appeared to be in her normal cheerful mood, smiling and patting Jack, who bounced up and down beside her until he received his fair share of attention, but Hilary decided that she had better be certain.

"Has everything been quite all right, Lucy? Has Lord Henry bothered you at all?"

"Oh, no, my lady. He has kept far away from us." She giggled a little. "And he looks ever so angry when he does see me. Even Branson leaves me alone now." Branson was the stocky footman whom Jack had bitten.

She patted Jack again. "No one appears to want to bother me with Jack there, and knowing that you would be angry if anything were to happen."

Pleased that at least one thing was going as it should, Hilary felt free to go about her business with an easy mind. She had been looking forward to this particular day. After attending a breakfast, she and Lily were going shopping, and Lily had promised faithfully that

Hilary could visit Ackermann's print shop for as long as she liked, for Lily had several errands to execute, and planned to end her excursion at Ackermann's.

Accordingly, after the breakfast at Lady Tilby's, Lily dropped Hilary at Ackermann's and proceeded on her way. To her surprise, Hilary found Lord Grayden had arrived there ahead of her and was engaged in inspecting their wares.

"I had no idea that you planned to visit here, too," she commented when he came over to make his bow. "Lily will not arrive until much later."

"Yes, I know," he replied. "When I heard you two talking about this yesterday, I decided that I would come to have a look around. I haven't been here in an eon."

He glanced around the tastefully arranged prints and screens and flower-stands and card-racks. Ackermann's sported a wealth of ornamental items for the home. It was, however, to the caricatures that Hilary was drawn.

Studying a merciless sketch of a pair of dandies "on the toddle" down Bond Street, she laughed a little reluctantly. "Perhaps my caricatures were kinder than I thought," she commented. "These would put mine to shame."

"These are more cruel," he agreed, "but I don't believe that they put your work to shame. Your sketches also have a vitality, a life of their own, and they offer an amusing insight into the person you are sketching. But you do it with a rapier instead of a broadsword."

"Thank you, sir," she replied, gratified by his assessment.

"In fact," he continued, "I think that you should consider showing some of your own work here. Your sketches would stand up against any of these."

Her eyes widened and she turned abruptly to stare

at him. "Show my work here?" she repeated, not certain that she had heard him correctly.

He nodded. "Unless, of course, you would not wish to do so."

"I had not even thought of such a thing," she said, stunned by the idea. "Do you mean that you think people might purchase them?"

"Certainly they would. People enjoy being amused, and many of your pictures do precisely that. I only regret that you destroyed the ones I saw at Drake Hall."

He smiled as he said that, and she suddenly realized that she had never before seen him smile as though he meant it. The effect was unexpectedly endearing. It was with some effort that she kept herself from putting her hand to his cheek and stroking it.

"I particularly enjoyed the one of Miss Brawley sitting in the mud puddle in front of her horse, the plume of her riding hat hanging damply over one eye."

Hilary laughed. "I must confess to you, Lord Grayden, that I did not destroy quite all of those sketches. I kept a few of them—and that is one."

"Excellent!" he exclaimed. "And I would be your first customer and purchase it."

"Yes, well," she said hesitantly, "but if I sell my work, won't that put me into—" She paused a moment.

"Into trade?" he said, finishing her question.

Hilary nodded.

"It is not at all the same thing," he assured her. "You are an artist, and you will not be doing the selling. You will not have to do any of the dealing in person. If you wish, my man of business will handle the sketches for you. In fact, you need not sign them with your own name if you do not wish to do so. You could maintain complete privacy."

"How very kind of you, Lord Grayden," she murmured. "I really don't know what to say."

And, for once, that was absolutely true. And, she thought a little resentfully, he had thrown her off-balance one more time, even though he had apparently done it from the kindest of motives. She had certainly never expected anything like this from Lord Grayden.

"Say that you will do it," he said encouragingly. "I will be more than happy to help, provided—"

He paused, looking at her with laughing eyes. She forced herself to ignore the warming effect of those eyes and to concentrate on his words.

"Provided that what?" she demanded, expecting the worst.

"Provided that I don't find myself the subject of one of them," he said.

She said nothing for a moment, so he studied her expression and then gave a shout of laughter, causing half the people in the room to turn and stare at them.

"You have already done it, haven't you, ma'am?" he demanded. "If I were to find that cursed sketchbook again, I should open it and see myself staring back at me—probably wearing a slab of beef where my head should be."

Hilary's cheeks turned the same shade as the cherries in her bonnet. She had not intended for him to know that she had made him one of her subjects, but she should have known that he would guess as much.

"I will not ask just how you have victimized me, Lady Hilary," he assured her, "but I most certainly would wish to purchase any sketch in which I appear, before it finds its way to a wider audience where I might be recognized."

Hilary's head was whirling. If Lord Grayden were correct and she truly could sell some of her work, she might be able to make enough of an income to support herself. Perhaps she might have an alternative to marrying Mr. Brawley after all. Of course, she had no notion how much one might make from such work, nor how much it would cost her to live apart from her family.

"Do you think that I—" she began, but broke off. She could not ask Lord Grayden whether he thought she could, as Clara put it, "earn her bread and butter" in such a manner.

He waited for her to finish, but when she could not, he said kindly, "Did you wish to know whether the gentlemen who create these make a living by it?"

She nodded gratefully, unable to meet his eye, however. A lady should never discuss such matters with a man not her relative, and assuredly she should not discuss something as crass as earning a living with any gentleman. Ladies and gentlemen did not talk about such matters and they did not "earn a living." Gentlemen who needed an income entered the church or the army, and ladies—well, ladies married and hoped for the best. Although, she had heard, a few wrote novels.

"I should imagine they can live quite comfortably," he observed. "And you do your sketches quickly, so being able to produce enough is not a problem for you, is it?"

Hilary shook her head, trying to stem the tide of hope that was breaking over her.

"How very kind of you to try to help me, Lord Grayden," she said suddenly. She was intensely grateful, but she was also, once more, astonished by his behavior. She would not have believed that he would have taken this much trouble on her account.

When she smiled into his eyes this time, she found it impossible to look away from the intensity of his gaze. How strange, she thought, that it was possible to have such an intimate moment in such a public place. She could focus on nothing except his eyes, and there seemed to be no barriers between them. The remarkable thing was that she was certain that he felt the same way. For a moment, she was certain that he was going to kiss her again, regardless of the fact they were standing in the middle of Ackermann's.

"Why, Lord Grayden, whatever are you doing here? And without Lady Carhill!"

The brittle voice of a fashionably dressed young woman with an equally brittle face broke the spell. The young woman looked curiously at Hilary, and the two companions who flanked her giggled, casting longing glances at Grayden.

"Good afternoon, Miss—Miss Morrison, is it not?" he replied, bowing to her.

Hilary had no doubt that he remembered her name perfectly well, but had blundered over it deliberately in order to inform her that she was not on an intimate footing with him. She had noticed that Grayden did not encourage familiarity.

"So good to see you," he murmured, bowing briefly once more before taking Hilary's arm and escorting her toward the door, leaving behind a red-faced Miss Morrison and her astonished companions.

"But I am to meet Lily here!" she protested as he steered her out onto the pavement.

"You know as well as I do that Lily will not appear for well over two hours, possibly three," he responded briskly. "In the meantime, I suggest that we take a quick ride through the park and then retire for refreshments. We must discuss your future."

Hilary felt as though she were treading on air. A sudden rush of gladness lent the day a glow, making even the autumn-nipped leaves on the trees more vivid. As they drove through the park, it seemed to her that a kaleidoscopic whirl of scarlet and orange and gold swept round her. So this, she thought, was what it was like to feel truly happy.

For a while they drove in comfortable silence, so that she had time to grow accustomed to the thought of freedom. It was almost more than she could bear. Her first coherent thought was that she should ask Lord Grayden to take her back to Lord Carhill's right away so that she could begin sketching. After all, the sooner she began, the sooner she could provide an income for herself—and perhaps even for Clara. She began to focus more carefully on the people they saw in passing, making mental notes about what her first sketches would be.

Lord Grayden watched her with interest. And he finally broke into her reverie, saying, "With your permission, Lady Hilary, tomorrow I will speak to Evans, who manages my business affairs."

"Oh, yes—yes, indeed you have my permission to do so, Lord Grayden. And you have my undying gratitude! This is beyond all measure kind, sir."

"I shall enjoy doing it," he responded, and she could see that he meant it. "Perhaps you could provide me with some samples that I could have Evans show," he suggested.

"Yes, of course I will. I can have those ready for you tomorrow."

"And shall you still be going to the Winters' rout tonight? Or will you be too busy with your work?"

She smiled. Her expression must be as revealing as he had indicated on their carriage journey to London. "You are quite right, Lord Grayden, that is what I would like to do. But I have promised Lily, and she is doing her best to help me, so I must not appear ungrateful."

She paused a moment, still thinking, then added mischievously, "I made myself sound so virtuous, didn't

I? To be honest, I will enjoy the evening—and who knows? I may find more material there."

"I am glad to hear it," he responded. "I wish for you to have as wide a range of choices as possible for your sketches. That may mean that you have less time to expose my foibles to the world."

Hilary looked at him directly for a moment, then said simply, "Thank you, Lord Grayden."

His eyes did not move from hers, and she once again felt herself slipping into a closer contact than she had ever known with anyone, even Clara.

The time drew out, until finally Grayden said in a low voice, "You are a dangerous woman, Lady Hilary."

Before she realized what was happening, they had leaned so close together that they were only inches apart. This time there was no Miss Morrison to break the spell, and she felt as though she was entering uncharted waters. When she once more glimpsed the tenderness in his eyes, she did what she had longed to do before, putting her hand to his cheek and stroking it. Grayden gently took her hand in his, lightly running his finger over her palm and the inside of her wrist, then kissing her palm and pressing it back to his cheek.

"You see what I mean?" he whispered. "Very dangerous. You make me forget myself."

A very nice way to put it, she thought dreamily, forgetting oneself, forgetting everything except the moment. The kiss when it came was tender but lingering, and Hilary straightened with a sigh when it was over.

Nothing more was said, but during the rest of the ride, he held her hand firmly, occasionally glancing at her reflectively. After a while, she grew restive, feeling that he was inspecting her.

"Why do you keep looking at me, Lord Grayden?" she finally asked, driven to it.

"I could say that it is because you are the most beautiful woman I have ever seen," he mused thoughtfully, raising an eyebrow.

"You could, but you would be telling a tale. That was not your expression when you looked at me."

"Indeed?" The eyebrow grew higher.

She shook her head emphatically. "Not at all. You were looking at me as though you were curious about something."

Grayden laughed. "That is why your sketches are so effective, Lady Hilary. You miss nothing."

"Well?" she prodded him. "What are you curious about?"

"I was wondering," he remarked reflectively, "just what you were trying to accomplish last night when you found me so beef-witted."

It was Hilary's turn to laugh, but she colored, too. She still could not tell him the entire truth of the matter, for it was not hers to tell. Certainly she could not tell him that she had been trying to lure him away from Lily so that she would pay more attention to Lord Carhill. So she told him a portion of the truth.

"Lily had explained to me how to charm a man," she remarked casually, "and I wanted to practice the lesson on you."

"Yes?" he said with interest. "And how did it work?"

"You know how it worked—or rather how it didn't work!" she replied tartly. "You are a poor subject for the experiment."

His laughter rang out once more. "Perhaps you weren't practicing the technique correctly. Tell me how it was supposed to go."

She explained it to him carefully, and as she had expected, he was once again highly entertained. "Is this how Lily believes she reels them in?" he asked.

It occurred to Hilary that Grayden took a very cavalier attitude toward Lily, whom he so faithfully squired. It also occurred to her that her own situation was a very curious one, but she decided that she would not worry about it just now. For the first time in her life, she was deeply happy.

At Gunter's she gave herself up to the pleasure of a lemon ice and conversation with Lord Grayden, and she made another delightful discovery. The two of them could talk, drifting from subject to subject, without reserve or boredom. Never had she felt such pleasure in another person's company.

By the time Grayden returned her to Ackermann's, the better part of the afternoon had gone, and he took his leave of her, promising that he would call for her and Lily that evening and reminding her that he would collect the sample sketches from her the next morning. Since they had both agreed that it would be best to keep the matter a secret, even—or perhaps especially— from Lily, she had arranged to send one of the footmen to deliver them to his house.

As she prepared for the party, Hilary carefully chose the gown she thought most becoming. After all, Lord Grayden might not think that she was the most beautiful woman he had ever seen, but she was certain that he found her attractive. She might as well make the most of her assets. And perhaps she did have a chance of engaging his attention so that Lily turned to her husband.

"You look beautiful, miss," sighed Lucy, as they completed her toilette. "You have a lovely color tonight."

"There's much to be said for being happy, Lucy," said Hilary. "I would like to try to make it a habit."

She had been completely wrong about Grayden, she reflected as she went downstairs to wait with Lily for him. She had thought him self-absorbed and frivolous, but he had been observant enough and kind enough to help her—to offer her a hope for her future that she had found from no one else. And, although she would not let herself quite believe that it was so, he appeared to be falling in love with her.

It had been, she thought for the hundredth time, the best day of her life.

Thirteen

To her pleasure, the evening also began delightfully. Not only did she have the attention of Colonel Hague and her normal attendants, but she also had the single honor of having Lord Grayden dance with her.

To her astonishment, he appeared at her side early in the evening and swept her onto the floor, ignoring Lily's outraged gasp.

"I thought that you did not dance, sir," Hilary remarked lightly. "I am glad to see that you have changed your mind."

"I have not necessarily changed my mind," Grayden replied thoughtfully. "I wish to dance with you, Lady Hilary, and I wish to dance tonight—but that does not mean that I wish to dance with anyone else. And perhaps after tonight I shall not dance again until I am quite an old man."

"And would you base that decision upon whether or not I am a good dancer?" she inquired. "If I should tread upon your toes, do you mean that you would renounce dancing for a score of years? If that is so, I can see that I had best be careful. I would have much to answer for."

He smiled. "No, my decision does not hang upon your skill as a dancer, ma'am, so you may rest easy."

"You relieve me," Hilary responded. "I am a fair dancer, but I would not wish to carry such a burden."

She looked up at him as they turned in a figure of the dance. "Upon what does your decision rest?"

He smiled down at her. "I fear that I must be unchivalrous and reply that I cannot tell you that, Lady Hilary—not at the moment, at any rate. Do you forgive me?"

Hilary shrugged, her own cheerful mood suddenly vanishing. Why had she expected him to continue the easy intimacy of the afternoon? That had been only a thing of the moment for him, the gratification of a whim. Across the room she could see Lily on the arm of another man but watching them closely.

Doubtless helping her with her sketches had only been a way to remove the pressure of worrying about her from Lily's shoulders. Grayden had always made that lady his first concern, so probably even dancing with her now had something to do with taking care of Lily.

"Of course I do," she replied shortly. "Your thoughts are your own, sir. I certainly have no right to them."

Grayden's smile faded at the abruptness of her tone. "I thought we were getting on rather better than that, ma'am. I'm sorry if I have offended you."

Hilary had the grace to blush. "Forgive my shortness of temper, Lord Grayden," she replied. "You have been most kind to me today, and I am afraid that made me feel that I had a greater right to your confidence than I truly do. I am the one in the wrong."

His response was not immediate, and she was finally forced to look up at him again, curious to see his expression. His gaze was as clear and close as it had been earlier, making her once again feel that they understood each other very well.

"I have already told you that you are a dangerous woman, ma'am," he said. "I did not fully realize just how accurate I was."

"Why do you say that?" she asked, puzzled. "I cannot see why that should be so. How can I possibly be a danger?"

"Do you not know that honesty can be most disarming? When Lily was giving you lessons in how to win the heart of a gentleman, I am afraid that some of her instructions were not entirely correct."

"How can that be so?" remarked Hilary, more puzzled still. "Just look at how the gentlemen flock around her. Why even Lord Carhill—" Here she broke off, for she had been about to add that even he and Lord Carhill, the two gentlemen she most admired, were members of Lily's court.

"Even Lord Carhill has given her his heart?" he inquired, his expression darkening. "I have noticed that you set great store by that gentleman, ma'am." He looked down at her. "What else were you going to add to that, Lady Hilary?"

"I'm afraid that I must take a page from your book, Lord Grayden, and ask that I also be allowed the privacy of my thoughts."

He inclined his head. "As you wish. I have no desire to intrude."

As the dance drew to a close, he led her back to their table and went in search of refreshments.

"Well!" exclaimed Lily sharply, when her partner returned her to the table and she took her place next to Hilary. "I am amazed that Grayden danced with you, Hilary! You must know that he never does so. Whatever were the two of you talking about? I saw that you looked very intent upon the conversation."

Hilary colored a little, but she managed to smile and reply lightly enough. "Oh, you know that Lord Grayden enjoys making sport of me, Lily. I daresay that he chose to dance simply to set some of the older ladies in a bustle. No doubt he wished to help me along by making me the subject of their speculation."

As though to confirm her words, Lady Gray bore down upon them, a fan of ostrich plumes in her hand and a wave of French perfume cascading before her.

"My dear Lady Hilary!" she exclaimed. "I saw you on the floor with Grayden just now! Why, I have not seen him dance for years, not since the first year he came down from Oxford. What a feather in your cap, my dear!"

Lily was beginning to look cross, and Hilary hurried into speech. "He was just taking pity upon me, Lady Gray," she assured the matron. "I can only hope that I did not tread upon his toes so many times that he will give up dancing altogether."

"Nonsense!" exclaimed Lady Gray. "He was enjoying himself hugely. I could see as much from where I stood! You were the envy of all the young ladies who have set their caps for him."

"You know that Grayden has no desire to marry!" said Lily sharply. "Why, he's shown no interest in anyone for years, at least not in any of the young ladies you refer to."

"You mean he has shown no interest in anyone save you, Lady Carhill," responded Lady Gray dryly. "And of course you are a married lady, and so it is perfectly safe for him to attend you."

Lily flushed, but before she could retort, the subject of their conversation arrived at the table, bearing refreshments for the two of them. Lady Gray turned to him and tapped him on the shoulder with her fan.

"I was glad to see you dancing again, Grayden," she said, smiling up at him. "It has been too long."

He bowed. "Perhaps, ma'am, you might do me the honor of dancing with me," he said. "I believe that I've not seen you take the floor this evening."

She laughed and again tapped him with the fan. "It would serve you right if I took your offer, you devil," she retorted. "As it is, I shall simply look forward to seeing you do so again." And she departed in a cloud of perfume.

"What a detestable old woman!" exclaimed Lily.

"Because she did not wish to dance with me?" inquired Grayden, looking at her with arched brows. "I had no idea that her refusal would upset you so, Lily."

"And you know very well that it did not!" she snapped.

"Then what did Lady Gray say to set your back up?" he asked.

Unable to think of a reply that would not cast her in a less than favorable light, Lily said nothing, but shrugged one shoulder pettishly and sipped her champagne. Lord Grayden caught Hilary's eye and smiled.

"And did Lady Gray upset you too, ma'am?" he asked.

Hilary shook her head. "She seems a very pleasant woman. She told me earlier that she and Lord Carhill were good friends when they were young."

Grayden nodded. "That is so. My mother was a friend of theirs, as well. I have known Lady Gray since I was in leading strings."

"Then you have known Lord Carhill that long?" asked Hilary.

He nodded. "He has been a good friend all of my life—none better. He is both my friend and my uncle. My mother was his sister."

Hilary sank into silence. For the moment the happiness that had returned to her during the dance appeared to be once more slipping away.

She could not deny that Lord Grayden was a most appealing man and that she was strongly drawn to him. Remembering Lord Carhill and Lily, however, she had to remind herself of the manner of man he was. He belonged to a world that she did not wish to understand, one in which a man could become the lover of the wife of a man who was both his uncle and his good friend. Clearly, there was the real Lord Grayden and the Lord Grayden she had conjured up in her imagination.

"Is there something wrong, Lady Hilary?" he asked with some concern, for he had been quick to observe the change in her expression.

"No, of course not. How could there be?" she replied, forcing herself to smile and sound lighthearted. "Everything is as it should be, is it not?"

"*You* may think so, but I certainly do not!" exclaimed Lily pettishly, glaring at Grayden. "I have an excruciating headache and wish to go home immediately!"

Hilary looked at her with some concern. Although she was quite certain that the headache had been brought on by her anger over Grayden dancing with someone else, Lily did look undeniably pale.

"Then we must go home immediately," Hilary said, rising from her chair.

"No, you sit down and enjoy yourself, Hilary," replied her friend. "Grayden will take me home. There is no need for you to miss the rest of the evening."

Grayden bowed to Hilary. "If you wish to stay, ma'am, please do. I shall be back immediately and will escort you home when you are ready."

Lily glared at him. She had not planned for him to leave her so abruptly at Grosvenor Square.

"Oh, then you might as well come along with us now, Hilary," she said crossly. "There is no point in having Grayden make two trips."

"I would be happy to do so, Lady Hilary," said Grayden quietly, ignoring Lily. "Please do as you wish in the matter."

"Of course I shall come now," she replied promptly. "I have no wish to be a burden."

Looking over the top of Lily's head at Hilary, Grayden smiled and took her hand, bowing over it. "You could never be a burden, ma'am," he assured her.

"Oh, do let's go!" exclaimed Lily. "I shall faint soon if we do not. The crush of the crowd is becoming too much for me!"

Well aware that the crush of the crowd would have been no problem if Lily had been the center of attention, Hilary gathered up her friend's reticule and fan and a pretty nosegay brought by one of her admirers.

The carriage ride home was a quiet one, and Grayden departed as soon as he had seen them into the house. Hilary made no attempt to cheer Lily or to turn her mind from her fancied grievance. There was never any point in reasoning with Lily. She simply had to have a little time to get over it.

The next day, all appeared to be normal again. Lily slept late, and Hilary had ample time to send a portfolio of her work to Lord Grayden before Lily appeared in the drawing room and Grayden came to pay his daily call. Eager to keep from further distressing Lily, Hilary studiously avoided engaging him in conversation, and he appeared to take that in good part, confining himself to a few general remarks and then departing.

At Hilary's suggestion, they then took a turn through the park. She had hoped that this outing would cheer Lily enough to keep her from spoiling the entire day. Also, she did not wish for Lily to go to see her husband in such a cross state of mind. Surely she could spare Lord Carhill that much, at least.

When they returned to Grosvenor Square, however, they discovered that there was to be no peace for either of them. The butler met them at the door with his eyebrows raised all the way to his hairline.

"You have callers, Lady Carhill," he informed her as he ushered them into the hall. "They insisted upon staying until you returned, so I took the liberty of showing them into the drawing room."

Lily paused at his words. "They insisted upon staying?" she responded. "What very odd behavior. I wonder who—"

She and Hilary suddenly stared at one another in dismay. "Did they give you a name, Jenkins?" demanded Lily.

He nodded. "I believe they said Brawley, Lady Carhill," he responded, his nose in the air. His opinion of the uninvited guests was clear.

Well, this would at least keep Lily's mind occupied for the moment, thought Hilary. However, it would also undoubtedly mean that she would be returning to Drake Hall very soon, before she had the chance to discover whether her sketches might be well received.

At that moment, the drawing-room doors were flung open and the Brawley contingent, not wishing to wait for Lady Carhill to come to them, impatiently descended upon her.

"*Dear* Lady Carhill!" chorused the ladies, enveloping her. "How very good it is to see you!"

"We came the instant we heard that dear Hilary was not recovering as she should!" said Mrs. Brawley, giving Hilary an accusing glance. "However, she appears to be doing well enough at the moment."

"Yes. She is doing somewhat better, but we just returned from a ride in the park to allow her some fresh air," said Lily, remembering her note to them. "I daresay that you are eager to take her back to Drake Hall with you."

The ladies and Mr. Brawley looked somewhat taken aback at her words.

"Well, of course we would not wish to be inconsiderate of Lady Hilary's health," amended Mrs. Brawley quickly.

"Naturally not," added Ophelia hurriedly, while her sister nodded vehemently.

Only Mr. Brawley looked dubious. "Since it appears that she is so much better, perhaps it would be best if we took her back to Drake Hall, where she can take the country air," he said.

The Brawley ladies glared at him. "You are too hasty, Raymond," his mother informed him. "I would ask you to defer to me in such a delicate matter."

Here she turned to Lily. "We have not yet had our luggage brought in, Lady Carhill," she said. "Your butler seemed to think that it would be best if we waited until your return before doing so."

Hilary looked at her friend in some distress. This was certainly more than Lily had bargained for when she rescued her friend. Once again, however, she had underestimated Lily's ability to deal with the Brawleys.

"He was quite correct to do so," replied Lily smoothly. "Lord Carhill is still unwell, and I have been careful to keep things quiet here. Grillon's, however, is an exceptional hotel, and you will be very comfortable there."

Seeing Mrs. Brawley about to protest, Lily held up her hand and smiled. "I know what you are going to say, madam, but I assure you that you will be able to secure rooms. Lord Carhill is well known there, and I shall send a footman around at once to notify them that you are coming. In fact," she added, scrutinizing the handsome grandfather clock that stood in the corner of the hall, "you will have enough time to rest a little before dressing for this evening."

"This evening?" responded Ophelia hopefully, swallowing her protests. "What is happening this evening?"

"Why, you will be joining us for Lord Montmorenci's ball," Lily responded cheerfully, "unless, of course, you are too weary from your journey today."

"No, not at all," Ophelia assured her, echoed by Deidre and her mother. "We would like it above all things."

Mr. Brawley allowed himself to be persuaded, and the Brawley troupe was finally escorted to the door and sent upon their way. As the door closed behind them, Lily leaned against the railing of the stairs and sighed.

"I was not certain that they would ever go," she said dolefully, rubbing her temples.

"I am so very sorry, Lily," said Hilary penitently. "I should have known that they would come, despite your sending them the note to hold them off."

Lily shook her head. "I should have expected it. I saw what kind of people they were at the outset. I could not have taken you from them so easily if they were not eager to make London connections."

"Not just any London connections," Hilary observed. "They wish to move in the first circles. Are you certain about the ball tonight, Lily? Should you have offered to take them?"

"It will be such a crush that no one will know that we have four extra people," Lily assured her. "The ball was our saving grace. It allowed me to send them to the hotel, and it will entertain them without our having to do anything."

The ball undoubtedly entertained the Brawleys, who were in their element. They did not allow not knowing anyone there to curtail their pleasure, and Ophelia and Deidre each managed to dance once. Both of them tried to secure Lord Grayden, but he proved too elusive, and they were forced to be satisfied with an unfortunate young man who fell into their hands late in the evening.

Hilary was sunk in despair as the carriage returned

home that night. Not only had she not had any opportunity for a private word with Grayden about her sketches, but she had also been forced to watch the performance of the Brawleys and to consider again the horrible prospect that she might be spending the rest of her life with them. The hope of winning her own way, which had arisen after her visit to Ackermann's, was receding. It had been a foolish notion after all, she told herself, based on nothing more than a young girl's dream. The Brawleys had brought her back to reality with a jolt.

It appeared that she would never again have the opportunity for a private word with Lord Grayden. The next morning she and Lily had scarcely gotten downstairs before the butler announced the Brawleys, who swarmed into the drawing room and made it their own. It was obvious that, although they might be residing at Grillon's, they planned to spend every waking minute possible in Grosvenor Square. Hilary stared at Lily in dismay.

One look at Lily's expression informed her that her return to Drake Hall was imminent.

Fourteen

The whole day was passed in company with the Brawleys. Although Lily and Hilary had planned to attend a dinner party that evening, Lily sent their regrets and they dined at home, complete with Brawleys, and then attended the theater, once again with the full Brawley contingent.

"At least they cannot talk through the entire evening," observed Lily bitterly. "Surely they will allow the actors their attention now and then."

And that, Hilary observed ruefully, was precisely the way it went. They indeed spared only desultory attention for the stage. The ladies talked incessantly, staring at the people in the audience and shamelessly attempting to capture Lord Grayden's notice. He remained imperturbable, occasionally answering one of their remarks and glancing now and then at Hilary.

Mortified by their behavior, she met his eye only once. Lily had said that he would not have gone to Drake Hall had he known the type of people he would be visiting there, and now he was being forced to endure their company, and to endure it in such a public place. She could not bear to see his contempt for them, so she studiously avoided catching his eye for the rest of the performance.

By the next morning, Lily had reached her breaking point. She and Hilary had gone down earlier than usual, in the hope of having a few minutes of peace before the Brawleys appeared. Lord Grayden appeared to be thinking along the same lines, for he too put in an early appearance.

"We must think of something to do with them!" Lily raged, as she recounted to Grayden the multitude of grievances she had against the Brawleys.

"Perhaps I should just go back to Drake Hall with them as soon as possible," ventured Hilary, who certainly wished to do no such thing.

To her dismay, but not to her surprise, Lily did not protest. Instead, she looked at Hilary hopefully. Before Hilary could reply, however, Lord Grayden intervened.

"Perhaps," he said quietly, "I have a better idea. Lily may not like it, of course, but it could at least relieve the pressure for a few days."

"If it will relieve me of the pressure of the Brawleys, I will like it," she assured him eagerly. "What is your idea, Grayden?"

"I will take them—and Lady Hilary, of course—to Endicott," he said smoothly, ignoring their startled expressions. "Since the Brawleys are shamelessly interested in forwarding their own interests with a person of title—forgive me for saying so, Lady Hilary"—he added, turning toward her for a moment, and she nodded—"no doubt they will leap at the chance. That will give you a little peace and quiet for your own activities, Lily."

"I cannot believe you just said such a thing!" exclaimed Lily, staring at him. "You know that you despise people like the Brawleys!"

Although she felt much the same way, Hilary remained silent.

"I believe that by doing so I can provide some relief, both for you and for Lady Hilary," he replied a little stiffly.

Lily did not take her eyes from his face. "Do you

indeed?" she asked in wonder. "Well, I cannot allow you to make such a sacrifice alone, Grayden. I shall go, too."

Hilary noted that Grayden looked somewhat less than gratified, though unsurprised. "Of course I shall be delighted to have you, Lily, and to have my uncle, too, if he feels himself equal to the journey."

"No, I think he would be tired by a day's ride in the coach. I shall come alone. Or perhaps I shall bring Henry," she added, glancing at Hilary. "At least then Robert will not be troubled by him."

Grayden bowed. "As you please," he responded, rising. "I shall make the arrangements immediately and we will leave tomorrow morning. I will return later this morning to extend my invitation to the Brawleys."

"Well, you may be certain you will find them here," returned Lily bitterly. "They look upon this as their home away from home. I am only surprised that they have not begun giving orders to Jenkins."

Lord Grayden refrained from remarking that she had known what she was getting into when she brought Hilary back to London with her, both because it would do no good and because Hilary had quite enough to withstand without his adding to it. He bowed to Hilary before leaving the drawing room, bidding her a good morning.

"I would never have imagined that Grayden would make such a sacrifice for me," mused Lily thoughtfully after the drawing-room doors had closed behind him. "His attachment to me must be even greater than I had guessed."

"Then you are a fortunate woman," observed Hilary crisply, "for he is making a considerable sacrifice by subjecting himself to the attentions of such a set of guests."

"Indeed he is," agreed Lily. "I can only hope that

he does not regret doing so." She turned to look at her friend. "How very devoted of him to try to shield me from such an experience."

Hilary nodded. "I am glad that Lord Carhill will not have to undergo it, but I do wish that he felt equal to the journey."

"Yes, of course," replied Lily absently, her mind clearly on other matters. "However, there is no point in risking his health—or, in this case, his peace of mind."

Hilary was of two minds as to how she should take that comment. Lord Carhill's peace of mind might possibly be overset by the behavior of the Brawleys, but she felt it much more likely that the threat would come from observing the closeness of the relationship between his wife and his nephew.

Later that afternoon, Hilary paid another visit to her host, and found Lord Carhill in excellent spirits.

"I understand that you are to visit Endicott," he observed as Walton made her comfortable and served their tea. "I believe that you will find it a most enjoyable experience."

"I am certain that I shall," she returned, smiling at his enthusiasm. "I only wish that you were feeling able to travel with us."

"I am most certainly doing better, as Walton will attest to," he replied, and Walton nodded as he served a slice of seedcake to each of them. "I almost believe that I could travel for a day without feeling any negative effects."

"That is good news," Hilary answered, her tone sincere. "Walton, would you please bring me the package that I gave to you as I entered?"

In a moment, the valet had retrieved the paper-wrapped package and Hilary had handed it to Lord Carhill.

"I had thought of giving this to you when I ended my visit," she said, smiling, "but I decided that now might be a better moment."

"A gift?" he exclaimed, carefully unwrapping it. "Why, I don't believe I've received a gift in a score of years!"

"Then it is more than time for you to have one," replied Hilary. How amazing, she thought, that such a generous man should have received so little in return.

She watched a little nervously as he turned the framed print toward him. It was the sketch that she had made of him and Lily strolling arm in arm along the street. They both sat in silence for a moment as he stared down at it.

"It is just the work of an amateur, of course," she said finally, "so please don't feel compelled to hang it. You will not offend me if you do not."

She waited, made uneasy by his silence, and she could see that Walton, hovering in the background, was also watching him. Finally, he looked up from the sketch and cleared his throat.

"It is a very happy scene," he said. "I shall hang it immediately." And he held it out to his valet, who hurried over. "You must put it where I can look at it often," he said to Walton, who bowed and smiled.

"I will see to it immediately, my lord," Walton assured him, taking it carefully.

"I meant what I said, Lord Carhill," Hilary said earnestly. "Pray do not hang it just for my benefit."

"It is not for your benefit, Lady Hilary," he said quietly. "I assure you that my motive is a selfish one. I shall feel happier each time I look at it and think of how my life could be."

"Of how it will be," responded Hilary firmly, watching his face carefully. "After all, you are doing much better than you were just last week."

Lord Carhill smiled at her. "Indeed I am," he agreed cheerfully, "and I cannot help but feel that you have much to do with that. You have been better than any medicine the doctor could have given me. I told Lily as much when she came up to tell me about the trip to Endicott."

"Do consider coming with us," Hilary urged him, encouraged by the fact that he was sitting up straighter and that his eyes were brighter. She thought of Lily spending time with Lord Grayden at his country home and felt that it was a great pity both for Lord Carhill to allow such intimacy and for him to miss such an opportunity to spend time with his wife.

For a moment his eyes grew brighter still, but then he sighed and shook his head. "Not tomorrow," he said reluctantly. "Perhaps I shall be able to follow you in a day or so. I have spent many happy times at Endicott. It would be a pleasure to have at least one more visit there."

"I am certain that there will be many more," Hilary said warmly. "Forgive me for leaving now, but I must go and prepare for this evening."

"Ah yes," replied Lord Carhill. "You are going to the opera, are you not?"

Hilary nodded. "It will be a great trial, I know," she said, referring to the Brawleys with some reluctance. "I am certain that Lily has told you how difficult Mr. Brawley and his family have been. I am more sorry than I can say that they have behaved in such a manner."

"You are not answerable for their behavior," he returned firmly. "Never feel that you are. At the moment," he reminded her, "you are not even engaged to Mr. Brawley."

He paused a moment, looking at her intently. "And you need not be. Please remember what I have said to you before. I want you to consider this your second home and to come to us whenever you wish, for as long as you wish."

"Thank you, sir," Hilary replied, her voice quivering slightly. Being treated with such kindness was not within her experience and she found it difficult to deal with—more difficult than the indifference of her own family or the outright dislike of the Brawleys.

She bent over quickly and kissed him on the top of the head, then, amazed by her own audacity, hurried to the door that Walton was holding for her. At the door she paused and looked back, smiling and lifting a hand in farewell. He lifted his hand and smiled in return, then the door closed gently behind her.

The evening was a painful repetition of their evening at the theater. She was horrified to hear Ophelia speaking to Lord Grayden in a manner that indicated not only that she felt herself to be on an equal footing with him, but also that she was certain of his fondness for her.

Ophelia rapped him on the arm with her fan and leaned very close to him, saying, "Come now, Grayden, why don't you take me for a stroll through the gallery? You know that you would prefer that to watching the performance."

Deidre was watching her jealously and Mrs. Brawley was regarding the scene with an indulgent motherly smile. Before she could speak, however—and Hilary was certain that she was about to lend her support to Ophelia—Lily rose abruptly and put out her hand.

"Grayden, do come with me. I fear that the air has become too close in here and I feel quite dizzy."

"Certainly, Lady Carhill," he replied, rising quickly. Bowing and glancing toward Hilary, he added, "If you will excuse us, ladies." And he hurried Lily from the box.

"Well, of all the nerve!" exclaimed Ophelia, her face turning red with indignation.

"Yes, I would say that it did take a considerable amount of nerve," agreed Hilary calmly. "Since Lord Grayden is known to be Lady Carhill's cicisbeo, you were quite audacious to fling yourself at him in such a manner, Miss Brawley."

"Fling myself at him?" Ophelia gasped, her eyes widening. "How dare you say such a thing to me, Lady Hilary? I suppose that you think because you have a title that you are justified in speaking to me like that!"

"My title has nothing to do with it," Hilary returned, unruffled. "Good sense, however, and good breeding tell me that such behavior is not acceptable." *In for a penny, in for a pound,* she thought to herself. Ophelia was already angry with her, so she might as well speak her mind.

Ophelia bore a distinct likeness to a fish removed from water. Her mouth rounded and she appeared to be gasping for breath. Her eyes, Hilary noted with interest, also appeared fishlike: protruding and round and glassy.

"I am certain that Lady Hilary does not mean to—" began Mr. Brawley in his usual pompous tone. He seized every occasion possible to voice his opinion and to guide those about him, whether they wished to be guided or not.

"Lady Hilary does indeed mean to!" snapped Hilary. "Your sister knows quite well that she would not be here were it not for me, and her behavior is embarrassing me beyond words!" *Well, not quite beyond words,* she amended mentally, and continued her diatribe. "If Miss Brawley had the least notion of what is expected of a lady, she would not have been doing everything short of proposing to a man who obviously has no interest in her!"

"Lord Grayden most certainly is interested in me!" exclaimed Ophelia, raising her voice above those on the stage so that members of the audience began to stare. "Why else do you think he has invited us to visit at Endicott?"

"Certainly not in order to fix his interest with you," returned Hilary grimly. More than anything she wished to tell Ophelia precisely why Grayden had extended the invitation, but she feared that Mr. Brawley might take offense and refuse to go. Hilary had no wish to return to Drake Hall a moment earlier than was necessary, and she also wished to see Endicott. She bit her lip with vexation as Ophelia watched her triumphantly.

"You see, Lady Hilary?" she said. "You have no answer for that, do you? Lord Grayden wishes for me to see his estate, and I have every intention of becoming Lady Grayden before too many more weeks go by. Lady Carhill is already married, and Grayden needs a mistress for his home."

The rest of the Brawleys stared at her with admiration, although Deidre's expression was obviously a compound of jealousy and anxiety.

Hilary sighed. Her hope of being able to remain in London by selling her sketches was fading rapidly. She had deluded herself by believing that such a thing might be done, and it assuredly could not happen overnight, even if it were a possibility. She had hoped that she would at least be able to enjoy the journey to Endicott, but the chance of that appeared to be diminishing by the hour.

That chance diminished even more markedly when she and Lily arrived home that evening. A muffled barking greeted them, and Lily turned to her, her irritation obvious.

"Can't you keep him from making such a stir,

Hilary?" she demanded impatiently. "He will raise the whole household if he keeps that up."

Hilary rushed up the stairs, fearing the worst. In an unoccupied bedchamber, she found Jack closed in the wardrobe with a partially devoured bone lying on its floor. Opening the door to her own chamber, Hilary scanned it quickly. Lucy was nowhere to be seen.

Jack, not standing upon ceremony, dove for the stairs. Hilary followed him rapidly, pausing only long enough to snatch up her riding crop. She had left Lucy packing her things, and the crop lay on a table near the trunk. Still somewhat fearful of other servants, Lucy waited until the late hours to take Hilary's clothes downstairs to clean and press them, and she always took Jack with her.

Following Jack as quickly as she could, Hilary indeed discovered Lucy in the kitchen. Lord Henry was stretched unconscious on the brick floor while Lucy pressed a cold cloth to his head and Jack sat next to him, growling throatily.

"What happened, Lucy?" Hilary asked, looking down at her maid's tear-stained face. "How did he get Jack away from you?"

"I don't know, miss," sobbed the girl. "I couldn't find Jack, and I needed to finish spotting and pressing your riding habit so that I could pack it for tomorrow, so I came down here by myself. I'd no more than got the flatirons heated and begun my work when I heard Jack barking. That's when I turned around and saw Lord Henry. Oh, miss, have I killed him? I hit him with one of the flatirons when he tried to grab me."

"Henry!" gasped Lily, who had finally reluctantly followed Hilary into the depths of the basement. "Whatever have you done to him, you wretched girl?" she demanded of Lucy, who sobbed even more desperately at her words.

"Wretched girl, my eye!" exclaimed Hilary wrathfully. "Just what do you think Lord Henry's business was in the kitchen, Lily? And why do you think he locked my dog in the wardrobe of a deserted chamber?"

Lord Henry was beginning to stir, and Hilary surveyed him grimly. "He is fortunate that Lucy grabbed the flatiron that had cooled instead of one fresh from the fire," she observed. "As it is, I daresay he will have nothing except a goose egg upon his brow."

She helped Lucy to her feet. "I'll leave you to deal with him, Lily. I should imagine he will not wish to see either of us, and we most certainly have no desire to see any more of him."

Fifteen

She was not destined to have her wish, however, for the next morning Lord Henry made one of the party that set forth for Endicott. Moaning and pressing a cold compress to his head, he rode in the coach with Lily and Hilary and Jack, while Lord Grayden rode alongside them. The jubilant Brawleys, delighted by the Carhill coat of arms on the doors of their vehicle, followed in a separate carriage—Lily had made certain of that—and the servants followed in yet another. The final vehicle in the parade carried the luggage for the group. All in all, the Brawleys felt with pride that they were part of a most impressive procession.

Somewhat to Hilary's surprise, Lily seemed quite excited by the journey. She had been only once to Endicott, but she detailed its delights to Hilary enthusiastically.

"The maze is particularly striking," she told her friend, who listened with interest. "I got lost in it once and Grayden had to come and lead me out, for I could by no means find the way myself."

"Quite a treat for Grayden!" observed Henry caustically, readjusting the compress. He glared down at Jack as though the terrier were personally responsible for his misery. "Perhaps you can take the damned dog into it this time."

Lily and Hilary ignored his muttering, but Jack, taking exception to his tone and his glare, growled throatily, his hackles rising slightly. Henry hastily drew back a little farther from the dog, and Hilary stroked her pet absentmindedly, listening carefully to Lily's description.

"And the prospect from my chamber was charming," Lily continued, quite as though Henry had said nothing. "I do hope that Grayden has placed me there again. The windows look out over the rose garden, and a small stream with a bridge runs through the bottom of it."

She sighed and leaned back against the cushions. "I understand that there is a fair going on nearby," she added thoughtfully. "They always have one there this time of year. I daresay that Grayden will escort us there if I ask him to do so. I think it would be charming beyond belief to visit it. I do so love the rustic life!"

"Of course you do," said Henry, the edge in his voice more pronounced than ever. "I can just see you with your little staff and a flock of sheep, leading them through the flowery meadows to join some shepherd. And just who do you have in mind for that part, Lily? Could it possibly be—"

Not wishing to hear what he would say, Hilary interrupted, pointing out the window and calling, "What is that I see in the distance? Is there a house afire?"

The other two craned to look out, then Henry said in exasperation, "It is some farmer burning leaves, ma'am! I should think that someone from the country would be able to tell the difference between the two!"

Disappointed at the loss of a reason to stop the carriage and talk to Grayden, Lily leaned back again and said dreamily, "I should love to be present at a bonfire. Perhaps I shall ask Grayden to take me to one."

"By all means," observed Henry bitterly. "Do ask Grayden to set fire to Endicott so that you may have the pleasure of seeing something ablaze. I can see that this will be a charming excursion—bonfires and country fairs." Here he paused and glanced at Hilary. "Of course, we need not go elsewhere to find country bumpkins," he added.

Hilary eyed him with contempt. "Better an honest bumpkin than a pudding-hearted loose screw!" she snapped, reducing both of her listeners to a momentary startled silence. Lord Henry turned scarlet but made no retort, choosing instead to close his eyes and moan, demanding a new compress.

"I had no notion that you could use such language," said Lily, regarding Hilary a little blankly.

Remembering in time that her friend would not think well of her for having friends in the stable, Hilary just shrugged and smiled. "Do tell me more about Endicott," she said.

Lily needed little encouragement, and she returned to a catalog of the delights of the place while Hilary listened with genuine interest and Lord Henry pretended to sleep, twitching with annoyance each time Lily laughed.

Finally, as she was completing a glowing description of the orchards, Lord Henry opened his eyes and glared at her. "Endicott isn't paradise, Lily," he snapped. "It's nothing to fly up into the boughs over as you are doing!"

Lily glared back at him. "If I choose to think it quite exceptional, I am permitted to do so, Henry. After all, I do have Greece and Italy with which to compare it."

Further irritated by this reference to the fact that he had not yet been abroad, Henry subsided into a sulky silence and stared out the window. Happily, Lily directed her gaze out the other window and appeared to fall into a reverie, thinking, no doubt, of Endicott—and Grayden.

Relieved by the reprieve, Hilary gave herself up to

enjoying the countryside. She and Jack gazed peace-fully out the window, Jack's tail wagging eagerly each time he caught sight of a flock of sheep.

It was late afternoon by the time they arrived at En-dicott, and all of them were relieved to retire early that evening. Even the Brawleys, eagerly looking forward to the delights of the visit, felt able to postpone a tour of the estate until the next day.

Always an early riser, Hilary dressed quickly and went downstairs, hoping that she would be early enough for a quiet stroll in the gardens. She had been able to see from her window that Lily's praise of the beauties of Endicott had not been exaggerated, and she looked forward to enjoying them in peace.

"Up with the chickens, I see," commented Lord Grayden, joining her in the entry hall. "And are you going out so early, Lady Hilary?"

She nodded. "I always enjoy an early morning walk," she replied, adjusting her cloak over her shoul-ders.

"What about an early-morning ride?" he inquired. "You are fond of riding, are you not?"

Surprised, she nodded, then glanced down at her gown.

"I shall wait for you to change into your riding habit," he said. "I can show you more of Endicott on horseback than on foot."

Hilary hurried upstairs to change. Although he was undoubtedly simply playing the genial host, she was eager to ride and to see the estate. It did not matter, naturally, that she would be in his company and that they might slip into the familiar closeness of other oc-casions. Nor that she might discover what the reception of her sketches had been. Simply having the opportu-nity to enjoy the splendors of the golden autumn morn-ing would be enough, she told herself. Over the years, she had learned well how to enjoy the moment without thinking beyond it.

She did not ring for Lucy, hurriedly dressing herself and pausing long enough in front of the glass to be certain that her hat was on straight. Jack was safely with Lucy, so she did not need to worry about him—or about Lucy—in this new place. Lord Henry was on unfamiliar ground, and she counted upon his having no desire to displease his cousin. So long as Jack did not feel called upon to search out the sheep, she felt that all should be well.

"You ride well, Lady Hilary," observed Lord Grayden after they had ridden in silence for a mile or two, both of them enjoying the quiet of the early morning.

"Thank you, sir," she responded.

"I should certainly not expect to find you seated in a mud puddle, your hat over one eye, after your horse pitched you off," he continued.

"You are too kind," Hilary said cheerfully, determined not to rise to the bait. "I have, as I told you, had my own share of spills. You just didn't see the earlier sketchbooks that recorded them, or at least what I think they looked like."

"No, but I should like to," he responded. "And so would Evans. He said that your sketches received a very warm reception at Ackermann's."

Hilary caught her breath. She had hoped against hope that he would say that to her, but she still could not quite take it in. Reining in her horse, she turned to look at him intently.

"Is that really so, Lord Grayden?" she demanded. "Or are you just being kind?"

"Inquire among those who know me," he advised her crisply. "You will discover that 'kind' is not a word often applied to me. I am merely telling you what Evans told me."

Here he smiled at her, the warmth of his gaze melting her doubts. "And I had told you as much myself, Lady Hilary. And I have done as I said I would. I have purchased the delightful sketch of Ophelia in the mud puddle."

Hilary laughed. "Please be certain not to put it where she might see it. My life is quite lively enough without agitating her further."

"So I have noticed," he replied. "And about those earlier sketchbooks, ma'am, tell me again. Shall I find a picture of you after an upset, perhaps draped across a hedge instead of sitting in a mud puddle?"

"I'm afraid you will not be permitted to see those, sir," she informed him, urging her horse into movement once again. "Some things must remain private."

"But you did take a tumble or two?" he persisted, following her.

"Yes, of course. Everyone does."

"Yet you still ride," he observed, pulling alongside her on the narrow path.

"Yes, of course I do," she replied, staring at him. "Why would I not?"

"Miss Brawley no longer rides," he observed. "Despite the fact she told me that she loves to ride, her sister informed me that she is afraid of horses."

Hilary laughed. "It should probably be the other way around. The horses should tremble when she comes near them. She has a heavy hand."

"And when you took your tumbles," he continued, "did you always get back on the horse immediately?"

"Naturally," she replied, a little surprised that he would ask. "That is what they say you must do if you are not to become afraid."

"And are you never afraid?" he persisted.

"Not of horses," Hilary said, smiling.

"And what are you afraid of, ma'am?" he asked, leaning closer to her.

Firmly she looked away and turned the conversation, pointing with her whip to a snug stone house in the distance. "That is a very attractive cottage, Lord Grayden. Is it a part of your estate?"

He nodded, turning his horse's head in that direction. "It belongs to Tom Tiller and his family. They've lived there for three generations. I intended to stop in and say hello this morning."

As they approached the cottage, the door swung open and three small, sturdy children tumbled out ahead of a smiling young woman, neatly dressed and wiping her hands on her apron.

"Good morning, Lord Grayden," she said, bobbing a curtsy. "There's a chill in the air this morning. Won't you and the young lady come in and warm yourselves by the fire before you go on?"

"Is Tom here, Priscilla?" he asked.

The young woman shook her head. "He's gone to the field to see about the mare, but he'll be back for breakfast. I hope you'll come in and stay a little, sir. He would be sorry to miss seeing you."

"And I'd be sorry not to see him," replied Grayden. He glanced inquiringly at Hilary, who nodded. She was rather eager to see the inside of the cottage. Her head was fairly spinning with the sketches that she planned to make when she returned to her chamber.

"Lady Hilary, this is Priscilla Tiller," he announced after helping her from her horse. The young woman bobbed another curtsy, and Hilary smiled at her. She was as sturdy looking as the three children clinging to her skirts, and she stood to one side as Grayden opened the door and shepherded all of them inside.

An old woman in a white cap sat in a chair close by

the fire, dozing peacefully until the clatter of the children caused her to blink.

"It's good to see you, Granny Tiller," said Grayden, his voice a little louder as he bent over her and took her hand.

The old woman smiled at him and nodded. "You look more like your father each time I see you," she said. "I would know you as his son if I saw you on the other side of the world."

"And that's where he's been, Granny, on the other side of the world," said Priscilla, still smiling. Turning to Grayden, she added, "And we're glad to have you home again, sir. We have missed seeing you ride by or stop to talk with us."

"And I've missed that, too, Priscilla," he assured her. "There is no ride I have ever taken that seems as beautiful to me as the one here at home, coming past your house and across the river to the village. The Continent has nothing to match it."

The young woman, though listening attentively and smiling at his words, was hard at work at the hearth, having filled two mugs from a pitcher, sprinkled in some spices, and then plunged a heated poker into first one, then the other.

Flushed from her labors and the warmth of the fire, she handed one to Hilary and the second to Grayden. "It's mulled cider, my lady," she said to Hilary. "It will help to take the chill off the morning."

And she was quite right about that, reflected Hilary after taking a swallow of the brew. Before she could reply, the door opened and a young farmer entered the room, calling out cheerfully.

"I knew that it must be you, my lord, when I saw the black hobbled at the door."

He bowed to Grayden, but Grayden shook hands with him firmly and presented him to Hilary. Then the two of them, followed by the children, adjourned to the stable to inspect the promising foal that Tiller was raising.

Hilary turned back to find herself being closely regarded by two pairs of bright, interested eyes. A little uneasily, she seated herself on the wooden bench indicated by Priscilla, still sipping the steaming cider.

"You have a handsome home and family," Hilary said at last, smiling at Priscilla. "You must be proud of them."

Priscilla nodded earnestly. "I am, my lady, I am. And I do wish you the very same, my lady. Lord Grayden is a fine man."

Hilary stared at her. "Oh, there's nothing between Lord Grayden and me. That is to say—"

She stumbled for words, but Priscilla said apologetically, "Forgive me for taking such a liberty, ma'am. Lord Grayden had never before brought a lady with him on his visit, and I thought that—"

"Don't worry about it at all," replied Hilary hurriedly. "I can see that it would be a very natural mistake."

"Well, I am that sorry it is not true," said Priscilla regretfully. "We have long hoped that he would find a wife and settle down."

Hilary herself wondered why he had not done so, but she did not think it proper to discuss the matter with one of Grayden's tenants, much as she longed to do so. She liked the earnest young woman and her pleasant family and home.

When they heard the men returning, Priscilla bent toward her and whispered, "Take this and put it under your pillow on All Hallow's Eve, miss. You will dream of the man who will be your husband and it will bring good luck to you. I will be thinking of you."

And she pressed a bundle of fresh rosemary, bound

by a scarlet ribbon, into Hilary's hand. Startled, Hilary took it from her without question.

"What are you thinking?" inquired Grayden as they rode away a few minutes later, turning their horses back toward Endicott.

"I am thinking that Priscilla Tiller is a very fortunate woman," she replied. And then, hurrying to establish a lighter tone, she added, "And I am most grateful for such splendid material for my sketchbook. I shall need the entire visit in order to do justice just to Priscilla and her cottage and family."

"Yes, I suppose you will," he replied, watching her thoughtfully as they turned toward Endicott again. "I hope that you can spare us a little of your time, ma'am, and not devote it all to your work."

She smiled. "Since I have brought the Brawleys down upon you, Lord Grayden, I assure you that I shall not abandon you to their none too tender mercies."

"You relieve my mind," he assured her. "I shall rely upon your support."

And support was surely needed, she reflected later, looking at the expressions of those gathered about the breakfast table when they returned.

"Well!" said Ophelia, when Hilary and Lord Grayden entered, still in their riding habits. "One need not wonder how you have been spending your time while the rest of us have been sitting here waiting for you!"

"Waiting for us?" inquired Hilary politely. "Surely you were not waiting for us before having breakfast?" Here she looked pointedly at the plates of the guests, all of which bore the signs of hearty dining.

"No, but we were waiting for your company," retorted Ophelia, pouting in what she clearly considered a charming manner, focusing her attention entirely upon Grayden.

"Forgive me," said Grayden, dropping easily into his

chair at the head of the table. "I had not expected you to be down to breakfast so early in the day."

Hilary glanced at the clock and then nodded in agreement. "I did not know that any of you arose at this hour."

"But of course I do," replied Ophelia promptly, still gazing soulfully at Grayden. "And I would have been down even earlier in my riding dress had I known that we would be going out. I assure you that tomorrow I shall be better prepared."

"I fear that I have a meeting tomorrow morning with my bailiff and my man of business from London," said Grayden hurriedly. Then he glanced wickedly at Hilary and added, "Lady Hilary, however, is an excellent horsewoman, and, since I have shown her part of the grounds this morning, she would be happy, I know, to ride out with you tomorrow."

It would have been difficult to say who was more annoyed, Ophelia or Hilary, but Grayden avoided the eyes of both ladies, concentrating studiously upon his breakfast. "Yes, I always do say that there is nothing like a brisk ride to sharpen one's appetite. I'm certain that tomorrow we shall scarcely have food enough to keep you after your ride."

"I shall not be riding," announced Ophelia stiffly. "I do not think Lady Hilary is properly equipped to squire me about an area that is unknown to her. I shall await your company, Lord Grayden. When you have time, I shall certainly look forward to riding at your side."

"And so shall I," chimed in Deidre, who earned an unpleasant glance from her sister.

Grayden looked anything but gratified at this news, but he managed to conceal his chagrin. Hilary applied herself to her breakfast, determined to ignore any further conversation on the subject.

Lily looked at both of them crossly. "Well, I certainly would not wish for you to feel that my wishes must be attended to," she began petulantly, "but I do think, Grayden, that if Robert had the least notion that you were not—"

"That I was not catering to your every whim?" inquired Grayden suddenly, with a striking absence of affection. "I do not think that is what Lord Carhill has in mind, Lily."

Everyone else looked up, startled by the unexpected abruptness of his tone. Lily stared at him a moment, scarlet-cheeked, then rose and left the room without a word. The others sat uneasily for a moment, then Grayden also rose, bowed to the others, made his excuses, and left the dining room.

A brief but significant silence filled the room.

"You see!" exclaimed Ophelia triumphantly, looking at Hilary. "I told you that he was not interested in Lady Carhill. And even if he were, since she is married, that makes no difference whatsoever! Lord Grayden is in need of a wife, and I shall do very nicely."

Here she paused and preened, smoothing her hair and looking more like a bird of prey than ever, Hilary reflected. The only thing that would have made the moment more oppressive would have been the presence of Lord Henry, but fortunately he did not put in an appearance until much later in the day.

Hilary enjoyed the remainder of her day, devoting herself to her drawing, except for two brief excursions into the garden for exercise and ideas. Knowing that she had found a market for her work filled her with a new zeal to capture on paper the new world that she was seeing.

She also wrote a brief letter to Clara, not yet sharing the happy news of the sketches, for she was not certain how Miss Dunsmore would regard that activity, but telling her that she was at Endicott and that she was very, very happy. Here she allowed herself a moment to imagine setting up housekeeping with Clara in a modest set of rooms in London. She concluded by writing that Lord Grayden was kindness personified, an accolade that would have astonished that gentleman had he seen the letter.

When she rejoined the others that evening, she quickly realized that she was probably the only member of the party who was happy. Sensing the heavy mood as soon as she entered the room, she glanced around the main drawing room of Endicott at the gathered guests. Ophelia, thin and predatory, had attached herself to poor Grayden, while Deidre clung closely to them. Watching the machinations of the other two women, Lily glanced at Hilary now and again with a fulminating eye. Lord Henry was toasting the toes of his evening slippers in front of the fire, blithely ignoring Mr. Brawley and his mother.

There could scarcely have been a less inviting group than the one that presented itself to Hilary. For a moment, she entertained the brief but appealing idea of pleading illness and retiring to her chamber, but she was quite certain that Lily would follow her there and extricate her so that she would not miss her share of the misery.

Summoning up what cheerfulness she could, she smiled at Lord Grayden as she entered the room.

"What a lovely blaze," she observed, looking studiously toward the hearth and avoiding his eye.

"I see that you are a born conversationalist, Lady Hilary," remarked Lord Henry acidly. "You really must get out of the country more often so that you can learn other conversational gambits. I daresay you will wish to talk about the weather next."

"No," responded Hilary coolly, before Lord Grayden

could remark upon his guest's rudeness, "I was about to speak of dogs, Lord Henry—small, persistent dogs—and perhaps follow that with a reference to flat-irons. I daresay that you would prefer that as an opening."

"Well, how very peculiar!" exclaimed Ophelia, who had not the slightest notion what Hilary meant. "You grow stranger every day!"

"I do, naturally, hold your opinion dear, Miss Brawley," Hilary replied briskly. "Nonetheless, I shall try to bear up beneath the pressure of your disapproval."

She saw the glimmer of a smile on Grayden's lips as he stepped toward her and extended his arm. "Shall we go in to dinner, Lady Hilary?" he inquired, ignoring Lily and leaving her to the enraptured Mr. Brawley, while Lord Henry was left to escort Mrs. Brawley. Ophelia and Deidre were forced to walk in unhappily together.

Hilary allowed herself a small smile as she took her place. How very satisfying it was, at least for the moment, to supersede them in importance and to know that they were jealous.

Chiefly, however, she allowed herself to savor the delight of success over dinner. Knowing that she was successful as an artist had opened up doors to opportunities she had never dreamed might be hers. A whole new world lay before her, and it was with satisfaction that she ate her dinner and enjoyed the company of Lord Grayden, the man who had made it possible.

Sixteen

As she prepared for bed that evening, Hilary felt that it was safe to say that she was the only one who had enjoyed the evening. Unperturbed by any negative remarks to her or about her, she had floated through the evening in her own cloud of delight, happily awaiting the moment when she could return to her sketching. When she reached her chamber, even Lucy and Jack seemed mildly out of sorts. When Lucy left, however, Hilary sat long in front of the fire, drafting sketch after sketch, while Jack lay protectively across her slippered feet, dozing gently in the warmth and rumbling occasionally as he chased rabbits in his dreams.

After she finally decided that she must go to bed and get some rest before dawn broke, she sat for a few minutes longer, ruffling through the pages of her work. Thinking of Lord Carhill, still in London and longing for his wife, she quickly drew one more sketch. Knowing how much he wished to be active once again, she placed him on horseback, looking toward the Tiller farm. In the distance, near the farmhouse, she added a distant feminine figure on horseback. How very suitable that he would be looking toward Lily, she thought. Perhaps by putting the Tiller home there, Hilary would bring him a little of their wholesome health and happiness.

As she finished it, she sighed, wondering if it would

ever be a scene enacted in real life. Perhaps concentrating on it would help to give it reality. With that in mind, she resolutely tore it from her sketchbook and set it on the chest beside her bed. Then she went to her desk and wrote a letter to Lord Carhill, telling him how much they were enjoying the delights of Endicott and how much they all—particularly Lily—missed his presence.

"If you are feeling well enough to travel, dear sir," she wrote in closing, "perhaps coming to Endicott, which I know you love, and enjoying the fresh country air would do you a world of good."

Placing the letter next to the sketch, Hilary determined that she would send it off immediately. Lord Grayden had said that he was meeting with his bailiff and that later he would be conferring with Evans. She would ask that Evans take her letters back to London, and she hoped that he would be interested in taking back a new collection of her sketches as well.

Pleased with her work, she went to bed and slept the sleep of the just, awakening only when Lucy opened the curtains and daylight streamed into the room. Before going down to breakfast, Hilary enjoyed the unaccustomed luxury of having tea in her own room beside the fire, ruffling through her sketches.

Carefully, she chose the ones that she would send back to London with Evans and slipped them into a portfolio, placing it on the chest that held the picture of Lord Carhill. Once again she stopped and looked at it, visualizing him as he rode past the Tillers and on across the narrow bridge that led to the village. Anything was possible, she told herself. After all, he already looked worlds better than he had when she had first come.

Breakfast that morning was a test of her good spirits, however. She prepared carefully, choosing a new gown of deep mulberry and brushing Jack's already glossy coat. The two of them walked briskly down the stairs, but as soon as they entered the dining room, where Mrs. Brawley, her daughters, and Lord Henry had already assembled, the trouble began.

"Well!" remarked Ophelia, her tone icy. "I am astounded to see you here, Lady Hilary. How is it that you are not out riding with Lord Grayden, looking over the estate?"

"Or, since Grayden could not ride this morning because of his business affairs, could you not be assisting him with those?" inquired Lord Henry in amusement. "I am certain that a young woman so worldly and experienced as you could be of invaluable aid."

"Perhaps you should just take your place at the head of the table," tittered Deidre spitefully, eager not to be left out of the fun.

But it was up to Mrs. Brawley to deliver what she considered to be the coup de grace. Drawing herself up to her full height, her thin bosom swelling, she said, "It is unfortunate indeed that some young women think that a title makes them superior to young women who are possessed of natural beauty and elegance of mind."

A ripple of amusement ran round the table, but Hilary ignored it, giving her attention instead to her breakfast and smiling at the young footman who had looked at her sympathetically as he drew out her chair for her.

"I daresay that Lady Hilary, obviously not having spent time amongst the members of the *ton,* is not aware of how rustic her manners must seem," observed Lord Henry, with the air of one determined to be just.

Hilary decided that she might reply to this, so, without directing her gaze toward Lord Henry, she replied, "And it is a matter of some interest to me to note that some who *have* spent time in such company appear to so little advantage, seeking their amusements among the servants as though fearful of young ladies who have the right to reject them in favor of true gentlemen."

A brief silence ensued, for the other ladies looked somewhat mystified, while Lord Henry's complexion turned an unbecoming hue. Before he could gather himself to respond, however, Franklin, the butler, entered and bowed to Hilary.

"Lord Grayden asks you to forgive him for troubling you at your breakfast, Lady Hilary, but he would be very grateful if you could join him in the library. With your permission, I shall have your breakfast brought in to you there."

"Of course I shall come," replied Hilary, arising gratefully as the butler nodded to the footman, who hurriedly began assembling her breakfast on a salver to carry to the library.

To her satisfaction, the door closed behind her on a stunned silence. The timing for her deliverance and their discomfiture could scarcely have been better if Lord Grayden had been lingering at the door, listening to their conversation.

"And so, Lady Hilary," said Lord Grayden after she had been settled comfortably by the library fire, her breakfast in front of her on a butler's tray and the doors firmly closed on the rest of the world, "I have just been with Evans, and he has brought me a purse with your earnings during the past week."

Here he handed her a small but heavy bag. She placed it in her lap and opened it cautiously. To her astonishment, it was filled with guineas.

Seeing her expression, Lord Grayden smiled. "I asked him to bring it in gold. I thought that you might enjoy the sight of it more."

When she did not speak, he added, "I understand

that your work has been unusually well accepted, ma'am. I congratulate you."

"Thank you," said Hilary, finally looking at him, her cheeks faintly flushed. "I know that I should be horrified to be discussing such crass matters with a gentleman, but I cannot tell you how much this means to me. I have no notion what things cost or whether this is anything more than pin money for most ladies—or whether I shall be able to earn enough to allow me to live without my father's assistance—but I am most grateful for the hope you have given me."

"I have enjoyed doing it," he replied, watching her expression with pleasure. "I knew that you would not wish to speak with Evans directly, but he would be most happy to carry out any command of yours. He will, for instance, take back any sketches that you have ready today."

"That would be wonderful," she responded automatically, rising to go to her chamber and collect the portfolio. "I have prepared some."

"I will have Franklin tell Lucy to bring them down," he said, touching her arm and returning her to her chair as he reached for the bellpull.

"Tell her, please, that they are in the portfolio next to my bed," she told him gratefully, settling herself by the fire once more. Jack, who had been displaced as she started to rise, curled up across her feet once more to anchor her in place.

"You have been more than kind, sir," she told him, as he took his place next to her, stretching his booted feet toward the fire and scratching Jack's head.

He nodded briefly, clearly not eager to discuss his role in the matter. "Remember that you have sworn to me that you will remove any unflattering caricatures of me before handing them over to Evans," he reminded her lightly.

"I shall burn them," she assured him. Then, glancing at him a little hesitantly, she put her hand into the pocket of her gown and drew out the letter she had written a few hours earlier.

"I hate to ask you for something more when you have already been so generous, Lord Grayden, but I have two letters to send, too. One would be posted to my old governess at Werrington Manor."

"Of course, Lady Hilary. And the other?" he inquired.

"Do you think that Evans could take this one back to London for me and have it delivered to Lord Carhill?"

Grayden accepted the letters that she handed him, his gaze still firmly upon her face. "It is good of you to think of him, ma'am. I am certain that he will enjoy hearing from you."

Thinking of Grayden's involvement with Lily and the fact that the letter he held encouraged Lord Carhill to believe his wife was pining for him, she flushed a little more and remained silent.

A few minutes later Franklin ushered into the library an awed Lucy, who clutched the portfolio nervously.

"Thank you, Lucy," said Hilary, holding out her hand.

Passing it to her mistress, Lucy managed a curtsy and said shakily, "I beg your pardon, ma'am, but I brought the loose one next to it. I wasn't certain whether I was to bring it, too."

In her hands she held the sketch of Lord Carhill on horseback, gazing toward Lily and the Tiller farm. Lord Grayden took it from her and studied it carefully, at last lifting his eyes from the paper and meeting Hilary's.

"That will be all, Lucy," said Hilary, smiling carefully to show the girl that she had not made an error by bringing the sketch.

After Franklin closed the doors upon them once more, Grayden glanced down at the sketch again, murmuring, "You take quite an interest in this gentleman, Lady Hilary. And I see no hint of caricature here."

"Anyone who knows him must be interested in Lord Carhill's welfare," she responded. "I would give a great deal to see him in good health and riding as he is in my drawing. I did not of course intend for that sketch to go in the portfolio."

"Naturally not. And who is the lady in the distance?" he inquired, his voice growing sharp. "Could it be that he is looking toward you?"

Astonished both by his tone and his words, Hilary stared at him, unable even to frame a reply.

At that moment, the door swung open abruptly and Lily entered the room, her look forbidding.

"I understand from the others that you have summoned Hilary here, Grayden," she said. "I could not imagine what the two of you had to discuss that would require such privacy, so I—"

Here she broke off, for she focused on the sketch still in Grayden's hands. Fortunately, Hilary saw with gratitude, the other sketches were still safely in the portfolio, which lay unobtrusively on Grayden's desk.

"Why, that is Robert!" she exclaimed, taking it from Grayden and studying it intently. "Did you do this, Hilary?" she demanded, throwing her friend a sharp glance.

Hilary nodded without speaking.

"Why ever are you sketching Robert?" Lily demanded. "And why do you show him riding when you know that he cannot do so any longer?"

"I was thinking that perhaps he might soon be able to ride again," said Hilary slowly, watching Lily's face.

Her friend showed no particular affection for the subject of the drawing as she stared down at it. But then, she thought, Lily was angry at the moment—angry that Hilary was closeted with Grayden and she had been excluded. She had a most proprietary air about him, which was to be expected, Hilary supposed, unfamiliar with the ways of women with their lovers.

"Pah!" exclaimed her friend, dismissing that hope with a wave of her hand. "Do not be putting thoughts like that in Robert's head. He will only be disappointed."

Here she paused a moment and looked at the sketch more closely. "And I suppose I am the lady that he is looking at in the distance," she observed.

"Of course," replied Hilary evenly. "Who else should it be?"

She did not glance toward Lord Grayden as she spoke. She was suffering from such a turmoil of emotions that she could scarcely think. Deftly, she transferred the purse from her lap to the side of the chair so that the folds of her gown hid it from sight. She had no desire to be subjected to more of Lily's inquisition. Suddenly, however, she realized that her letter to Lord Carhill lay in clear sight, and she froze.

Unfortunately, Lily noticed her expression and followed her gaze, pouncing on the letter. "A letter to Robert!" she exclaimed. "And in your handwriting, Hilary! Why, pray tell, are you writing to my husband?"

"Simply to tell him that Endicott is all that he described it to be," Hilary replied slowly. "And to tell him that we miss his presence."

"I shall write one myself," announced Lily. "That is the wife's duty—to write to her husband and tell him that he is missed."

"I know that he will be happy to hear that you miss him," Hilary said sincerely.

At least, she reflected, one good thing was coming

of this unpleasant episode. She knew that Lord Carhill
would be delighted beyond measure to hear from
Lily—and that Lily would never have thought of writing unless she had been goaded into action.

"Do not let his affection for you go to your head,
Hilary!" said Lily sharply. "Pray remember that he is
still *my* husband!"

Hilary stared at her friend's angry face, stunned by
her words. "His affection for me?" she replied blankly.
"What are you talking about, Lily?"

"Don't play the innocent with me, my girl! I had not
thought you so worldly wise nor so ungrateful as to try
to worm yourself into his affections while he is ill! It
is always 'Hilary this!' and 'Hilary that!' until I am
quite sick of hearing it! Why, he even told me that you
have been better for him than any medicine could have
been!"

Hilary remained frozen in place, unable to take in
what Lily was saying. Lord Grayden merely observed
the exchange without saying a word.

Finally, Hilary managed to gather her wits enough
to say, "You know that what you are saying is foolish
beyond permission, Lily! Lord Carhill has been kindness itself to me, but I certainly have not tried to—as
you say—*worm* myself into his affections. I have enjoyed his company and I merely wished to act the part
of a friend."

"A friend!" exclaimed Lily. "You are supposed to
be *my* friend, Hilary, and yet you write notes to my
husband and spend time with him to try to supplant
me in his affections!"

"I have done no such thing, Lily!" replied Hilary,
her indignation growing at this unwarranted attack.
"And even if you would think such a thing of me, you
should have better sense than to suppose such a thing
about Lord Carhill!"

"Ah yes, I forget that you understand him so much better than I," retorted Lily.

She had seated herself at Grayden's desk, pushing the portfolio out of the way and rifling through the drawers, tossing papers helter-skelter as she looked for stationery.

"Wherever do you keep things, Grayden?" she asked petulantly. "I don't see anything I need to write to Robert."

"By all means, Lily, let me assist you," he answered patiently, placing before her paper, pen, ink, and blotter and trying to restore some order to the contents of his desk. "I will seal it for you when you have finished, and Evans can carry it back to London and deliver it for you."

"Very well," murmured Lily, scribbling hastily. "There!" she said a minute later, having written no more than four or five lines. "I am finished!"

As Grayden folded it and stamped the hot wax with his seal, she rose from the chair and paced back and forth.

"Really, Grayden, you must do something!" she said, pressing her hands to either side of her brow.

"Just what must I do something about?" he inquired, hoping that she was not about to take up her attack once more. "Do you have the headache, Lily? Should I have Franklin bring you some *sal volatile?*"

She waved her hand at him impatiently. "Smelling salts will do no good," she assured him. "Not only must I worry about Hilary and Robert! No, that is not enough of a burden for me to bear! I must also be subjected to those encroaching Brawleys! How am I to endure them?"

"Lily, if you recall, the reason that the Brawleys are here is so that you would be spared their presence in

London," he reminded her reasonably. "You could be home in London with Robert and free of the Brawleys."

Listening carefully, Hilary considered this an interesting point, but she knew that Lily would have gone anywhere that Grayden was going if it were possible. Her jealousy over Lord Carhill was simply because of her possessiveness. He was not to be allowed to admire any lady other than his wife, but she was free to bestow her affections where she pleased.

"Yes, yes, I know, Grayden!" she replied, her voice growing more petulant by the minute. "But I could not let you face them alone."

She ignored Hilary as though her friend did not exist. "I cannot think how anyone can be expected to bear them for more than thirty minutes!"

For a moment Hilary thought of a lifetime with the Brawleys, and the room grew dark. Then she felt the comforting weight of the purse filled with guineas, and she took a deep breath. If she could only have a few weeks to gather at least a little money, she would not allow her father to make her the family sacrifice.

"Perhaps, Lily, it will help you to know that we shall have guests for dinner this evening, and a few more coming in after dinner to spend the evening."

Lily's expression lightened immediately. "And shall we have dancing, Grayden?" she asked, allowing herself to be diverted.

"Of course," he responded, bowing. "I knew that you would like that above all things."

"Yes, indeed, Grayden," Lily said, taking his hand gratefully and holding it to her cheek for a moment. "You are far too good to me."

"I prefer you happy," he said lightly, although he did not appear amused. "For when you are unhappy, Lily, none of us have any peace."

"Ah, you are always teasing, Grayden, but I know

that you would do anything for me!" she exclaimed, her mood now as gay as it had been petulant a few moments earlier.

Here she reached up and cupped his face in her hands, pulling him down toward her so that she could plant a dainty kiss on his cheek. Without another word to Hilary, she tripped lightly from the room, pulling him with her to announce the party to the others.

Left to consider the implications of Lily's rancor, Hilary sat for a long while in the library. Finally, reminding herself that she had at least made a beginning on a new future with her purse filled with guineas, she picked it up and returned slowly to her chamber, deliberately blotting from her mind the picture of Lily kissing Grayden and leading him so possessively from the room.

Seventeen

The dinner party was not a resounding success, even for the Brawleys. For them, it was indeed an evening of pleasure because they were the companions of Lord Grayden and his neighbors, and they reveled in this closeness to the peerage, finding it much more pleasurable than the company of Lady Hilary.

Nonetheless, Ophelia was unable to persuade Lord Grayden to stand up with her, and she was forced to make do with a young man two years her junior for the majority of the dances. Deidre for once outdid her sister, for her squire for the evening was a good-natured gentleman some forty years her senior. She preened herself upon her conquest extensively, pointing out to Ophelia several times during the course of the evening that Colonel Lloyd was the second cousin of an earl. Mrs. Brawley frowned to see that her daughters were not properly appreciated, and Mr. Brawley unfortunately chose this evening to share with Hilary his disapproval of her behavior.

He insisted on leading Hilary out to dance twice, which was twice more than she wished. After the second dance, instead of escorting her to a chair and bringing her refreshments, he led her to the library.

"Is there something wrong, Mr. Brawley?" she inquired, her brows arched, as he closed the door behind them.

Not waiting for him to reply, she walked over to the door and opened it, leaving it standing ajar. Then she turned to face him, fully aware that her height intimidated him.

"Please be seated, Lady Hilary," he said, indicating a chair.

"I do not wish to sit down, sir," she answered. "I wish to return to the others, so unless you have some pressing matter to discuss—"

"But I do," he interrupted gravely. "Much as I dislike doing this, I fear that I must."

For a moment her heart leaped with joy. He was going to tell her that they would not suit, that they would not be married. She would not need to tell her father that she would not marry Brawley; he would tell her father himself. It was with some difficulty that she kept from smiling.

"And what is it that you so dislike doing?" she asked encouragingly. He must not be allowed to change his mind.

"I must ask you, Lady Hilary," he said in measured tones, sounding as pompous as he normally did, "to consider your behavior more carefully in the future and to remember that what you do must reflect upon me."

Hilary stared at him in astonishment.

Seeing with approval that she was taking this matter seriously, he continued, "I realize that you are young and inexperienced, in spite of your two Seasons in Town, so I can make allowances for you."

"How very kind of you," she remarked dryly, regaining her power of speech and looking at him with active dislike. "May I ask just what I have done that you feel you cannot condone?"

He looked at her in surprise. "Why, closeting yourself privately with Lord Grayden this morning was scarcely maidenly behavior, Lady Hilary. Nor was riding out alone with him, without even a groom, a judicious decision. I can see that you need a guiding hand, one more forceful than your father's has been."

"I am afraid, Mr. Brawley, that I do not feel that you have the right to say these things to me. And most certainly you have no right to attempt to guide my behavior and put yourself in place of my father."

"But you know, Lady Hilary, that we are to be married," he replied, drawing himself to his full height and looking at her in amazement.

"I do not know it," she assured him. "No contract has been made, nor have you asked for my hand. At the moment, we are nothing more than acquaintances."

Hilary strode to the door, turning back to look at him once more before leaving.

"And if you will look about you, Mr. Brawley, you will see what a gentleman's library should look like. There should be books upon the shelves that are not only readable, but that have actually been read. Perhaps you should soothe your feelings by reading a little philosophy before returning to the party!"

She slammed the door behind her.

Nor was Lily particularly happy with the evening. Not only were the Brawleys very much present, their attentions to Lord Grayden annoying her beyond the telling, but Grayden himself seemed more distant than usual. When she tried to engage him in conversation, he answered in monosyllables, and none of her flirtatious sallies brought a twinkle to his eye.

Nor could she look at Hilary without feeling a wave of anger wash over her again. So ungrateful of Hilary to try to usurp her place with Robert and even to try to occupy Grayden's attention. The girl was getting too far above herself. Lily allowed herself the indulgence of self-pity as she thought of what she had done for Hilary, only to be treated so unkindly in return.

Poor Grayden felt like a beast at bay, being stalked by the Brawleys and by Lily. He watched Lady Hilary thoughtfully during the course of the evening, wondering just why she had made such an effort to be close to Lord Carhill. Although he recognized Lily's jealousy for what it was, he was not absolutely certain of Hilary's motives. He knew, however, that his uncle most certainly held her in high regard.

It was possible, he thought reluctantly, that she had considered a way other than her drawing to keep herself from becoming the wife of Mr. Brawley. And after an enforced closeness with that gentleman, he was inclined to feel that she might be justified in taking such a step. Still, he would be sorry to think that she might stoop to attaching Lord Carhill's affections with such an end in mind.

Hilary watched the majority of the events of the evening with a grateful eye, grateful because the Brawleys were, for the most part, happily employed and more grateful still that she had so much new subject matter for her sketches. When, upon that lady's loud insistence, Lord Grayden danced once with Lily, she did not pay strict attention to their performance, for she stood up herself with an elderly gentleman who had the sprightly dancing habits of a grasshopper and who made her heart grow lighter as she watched him. He would, she thought, be an excellent subject for her art.

When that gentleman had come over to ask her to dance, she had not been able to resist him. As he led her onto the floor, he said, "You must be aware, Lady Hilary, that you are the loveliest young woman at this affair. If I were a young man, I should ask for your hand in marriage immediately. I am astonished that you have not been snatched up."

Hilary laughed. "I am afraid that not everyone would

agree with you, Mr. Elliott," she replied. "As you can see, there are no scores of young men waiting for me."

"Then they are fools," he said briskly, going nimbly through the figures of the dance. "And they will be sorry for it by and by. Do not you mind them, my dear. After all, you would not wish to marry a fool."

Thinking of Mr. Brawley, she was forced to agree with Mr. Elliott. Most certainly, she would not wish to marry a fool.

As he led her back to her place, Mr. Elliott said, "If you are going to be at Endicott a little longer, be certain that you have Grayden take you to the horse fair in the village. It is the big event of our year, and you would find it amusing, I think."

Hilary's eyes lighted at the thought of so many new scenes. She had quite forgotten Lily's mention of a fair, and she thanked Mr. Elliott profusely for reminding her of the event. She was determined that they would go, for such a visit would provide her with a wealth of material for her work. Now that the opportunity of a career had presented itself, she found that she saw everyone and everything as a potential sketch.

As Mr. Elliott left her, she saw Lord Grayden approaching.

"I am afraid, Lady Hilary, that in the excitement of the events of the morning, I forgot to give you a letter that came to you in London. Evans brought it down with my other mail. I apologize for my oversight."

Here he handed her a small letter, and she recognized Clara's copperplate handwriting.

"Thank you," she murmured, slipping from the crowded room so that she could read it in peace. She had noticed that Clara's usually immaculate writing was a little askew, which meant, she knew from experience, that the governess was writing under great stress.

She returned to the quiet of the library and read Clara's missive by the fire. It was as she feared. Lord Werrington had chosen this time to give Miss Dunsmore her notice, telling her that she would be of little use to them now that Hilary would be getting married and their youngest son was being sent to school.

> *"Lord Werrington seems to feel, however,"* Clara wrote, her script becoming shakier still, *"that I might find a home with you if Mr. Brawley found that acceptable. Perhaps—forgive me for saying this, my dear Hilary—perhaps looking ahead to the children that you would have. At any rate,"* she continued, *"I shall be leaving Werrington Manor at the end of the month, and I shall be in touch with you. Do not feel, dear child, that you must take any responsibility for my welfare. I am certain that I shall find a position very soon."*

Hilary stared into the fire angrily. How very like her father to do this while she was gone! And now, in order to rescue Clara, she would have to agree to marry Brawley. She would have to abase herself and apologize and grovel to him, begging him to take in her elderly governess as well. And she would have to do it, she knew, because there was no way that she could take care of Clara and herself through her drawing at this time. Nor could she let Miss Dunsmore go virtually penniless into the world. Her father, she knew all too well, would do nothing to help her.

Hilary's anger grew until the room became too hot for her, and she slipped from the house, opening a side door and walking out into the rose garden so that she could be alone. After a few turns through the chilly, moonlit garden, however, she discovered that she had company.

"Lord Grayden!" she exclaimed, as he appeared suddenly beside her. "I did not hear you approaching."

"Forgive me, Lady Hilary, I didn't mean to startle you, but I brought you a wrap. It is colder out here than you might at first suppose."

Hilary accepted the warm shawl gratefully, wrapping it about her shoulders and staring up at the moon, its orange globe almost full. She had done her best to place the problem of Clara into a compartment, waiting to deal with it tomorrow. For the time, she would concentrate on the moment.

"A harvest moon," she remarked idly. "Precisely what we should be seeing at this time in the country. Did you order it especially for the evening, Lord Grayden?"

"Naturally," he responded, gazing at her instead of the moon. "Some are fonder of a golden moon, but I feel that the richness of this shade puts the other to shame. Do you not agree?"

She murmured her assent, happy for the moment merely to be safely away from the Brawleys and to be enjoying his company. For just this little time, she would not think about Clara or about Lily—or about Grayden's betrayal of Lord Carhill. Instead, she would allow herself a little happiness. Surely she deserved that much.

She knew without speaking that he was as keenly aware of her as she was of him, so it was no surprise when he suddenly drew her close and kissed her, wrapping her warmly in his arms and kissing her deeply.

In the midst of it, however, a sudden vivid picture of Clara, crying over her letter and fearing the future that held no place for her, washed over her. She drew sharply away from Grayden, the vision of Raymond Brawley rising before her like a conjured spirit.

"What is it?" he asked gently, smoothing the curls from her face and finding the traces of tears there. "What is troubling you?"

"I must marry Brawley," she said briefly, not looking at him.

"Why even consider marrying Brawley?" he whispered, pulling her close to him again. "Think of all that you will miss if you marry a man like that. You have seen today that your drawing will earn at least some money for you. Do you care so much for money that you must still marry him?"

"You obviously have never had less than enough money yourself, sir, or you would not ask!" she responded sharply, pulling away from him and turning toward the house.

Lily met her just inside the door, small and rigid with anger.

"I saw you in the garden with Grayden just now!" she said. "You are indeed shameless, Hilary! You attempt to ensnare Robert, and now you fling yourself at Grayden. You must leave Endicott tomorrow and take the Brawleys with you!"

"I quite agree," said Hilary quietly, walking past her and up the stairs without a backward glance.

After she dismissed Lucy that night, Hilary took from a drawer the rosemary Priscilla Tiller had given her and set it in her lap to look at it. It was nothing more than superstition of course, and Priscilla's wishful thinking, but it was a charming thought and the rosemary was lovely to look at, bound brightly in its scarlet ribbon. She sketched it sadly. All Hallow's Eve was fast approaching, and she had had every intention of tucking the rosemary under her pillow on that night. After all, one never knew. Now, of course, there would be no point in it. Her future would be determined as soon as she abased herself to Mr. Brawley the next morning.

Even Jack, sensing her unhappiness and lying firmly across both her feet, could offer no comfort. Her future with the Brawleys looked even bleaker now than it had, for she had had a glimpse of freedom and knew now what she would be missing. Still, she had Clara to provide for, and certainly her art had offered no guaranteed future.

The night was a restless one, and sleep was long in coming. Hilary felt as though she had scarcely touched her head to the pillow when Lucy entered the chamber, opening the curtains and bringing her hot water to wash.

Hilary lay there with her eyes closed, listening to the little maid go about her morning business, but she was aware of a sudden sharp stillness.

"Lady Hilary! Forgive me for waking you, miss, but—"

"What is wrong, Lucy?" Hilary asked, opening her eyes at her maid's urgent tone. "Has something happened?"

"Where is Jack?" asked Lucy. "His basket is empty."

Hilary sat up abruptly, attempting to clear her mind. Jack! He had been here last night, for she had had to move him from her feet and place him in the basket next to her bed. While she had tossed and turned, he had been restless, too, pacing back and forth and whining, but she had attributed that to the fact that she could not sleep. She had certainly not opened the door and let him out.

Together they searched under the bed and inspected the wardrobe and scoured the room for any clues. Jack was not there, nor was there the least sign of what had happened to him.

"I'll call him," said Hilary, going to the door of her chamber.

"Lady Hilary! You are still in your nightgown!" exclaimed Lucy, scrambling to find her mistress's dressing gown.

"Don't bother with it, Lucy," she said, opening the door. She stepped into the corridor and called Jack's name, then stood listening. There was no answering bark. She tried once more, but to no effect.

The only reaction she received was Ophelia opening the door of her chamber and exclaiming waspishly, "Must you be so ill-bred, Lady Hilary? Some of us are still trying to sleep!"

Hilary made no reply, but hurried back into her room to dress.

"I must search the house," she said as Lucy helped her. "And I'll go down to the stable. Jack is fond of horses, and the stableboys are always glad to see him."

"I'll go down to the kitchen, miss, and ask if Cook or any of the others have seen him."

As soon as she had put Hilary to rights, Lucy scuttled from the room, heading for the belowstairs area belonging to the servants. Jack enjoyed the favor of the cook, so it was possible he might have taken himself down in the hope of receiving a breakfast sausage.

The cook, however, had not seen him, nor had the other servants. When she reported her failure to Hilary, who had fruitlessly searched the rest of the house, Lucy added one afterthought.

"That Marie of Miss Brawley's always acts as though she knows more than she does, Lady Hilary, so I daresay it does not amount to anything—"

"What does not amount to anything, Lucy?" demanded Hilary. "What did Marie say?"

"It isn't that she exactly said anything, miss," replied Lucy slowly. "It was more that she acted as though she knew something when I asked if anyone had seen Jack. The others said they hadn't, but Marie just smiled and sort of pressed her lips together as though she *could* say something but wouldn't."

"Well, we'll find out about that soon enough!" replied Hilary grimly, ringing for Franklin and asking him to send Miss Brawley's abigail in to speak with her.

Marie still looked at Hilary as insolently as ever, although she appeared to lose a little of her assurance when Franklin left her in the drawing room.

"Marie, do you know where my dog Jack is?" inquired Hilary, taking the direct approach.

Marie lifted one shoulder. "How would I know anything of your dog, miss?" she inquired. "I am not your maid nor do I keep a kennel."

"It would be as well for you to keep a civil tongue in your head, my girl," replied Hilary, rising to her feet and staring down at the maid, who began to look still less assured. "And if you have the least notion where Jack might have gotten to, you would be wise to tell me now, or I shall have Lord Grayden take steps to look into this matter with you himself."

"He is not my employer," retorted Marie, still game but sounding weaker by the minute.

"And do you seriously think that Miss Brawley would not do whatever Lord Grayden wished her to?" asked Hilary sternly. "If he advised her that she would be better off with a maid who told the truth, I daresay that she would listen to him and that, my girl, would be the end of you. You would be turned off without a reference."

At this, Marie began to grow pale. She knew all too well how infatuated Miss Brawley was with Lord Grayden, and she was aware that Lord Grayden appeared to be fond of Lady Hilary. Suddenly she felt less secure of her ground.

"I will tell you what I know, miss, but it isn't much," she replied, crumbling suddenly as she envisioned a future with no job and no letter of reference.

"I am listening," said Hilary, standing close to her so that she would not change her mind and leave the room.

"It was Lord Henry," said Marie in a low voice.

It was Hilary's turn to grow pale. "What about Lord Henry?" she asked evenly. "What does he have to do with Jack?"

"He told me to go to your chamber and open the door a crack late last night. I was to slide in a dish of food he gave me and shut the door again. I was to wait an hour or so, then go back again and get both the food and the dog."

"Poison!" exclaimed Hilary, her eyes flashing as she stepped nearer the girl. "Did you poison my dog, Marie?" she demanded.

Marie backed away from her, truly frightened now. "No, miss! I swear the dog was alive when I carried him out. He was asleep—Lord Henry must have drugged him—but he was breathing."

"And where did you take him?" Hilary asked, her eyes cold.

"To Lord Henry's chamber, as I was told to do," Marie answered sulkily. "I only did as I was bid, miss."

"Yes, but you knew that what you were doing was wrong," responded Hilary. "Do you know what Lord Henry did with Jack after that?"

Marie shook her head firmly. "No, miss. It was late and I went to bed. I didn't want to spend any more time on a dog, and I wouldn't have done that unless—"

"Unless what?" demanded Hilary. "Did Lord Henry pay you?"

Marie nodded. "He told me that if no one found out about it, he would give me ten pounds more."

She looked at Hilary a moment. "But I don't suppose I'm going to get that ten pounds," she remarked.

"Indeed you are not," said Hilary, "for Lord Henry is about to be made keenly aware that someone has found out about it."

"May I go now, miss?" Marie asked, edging toward the door.

Hilary nodded grimly, her attention now turned to her course of action. She would go to Lord Henry's chamber, she decided. That was where Marie had taken Jack, and with any luck, he might be there still, too drugged to respond to her calling.

Eighteen

After knocking several times at Lord Henry's door, Hilary, with Lucy at her heels, took a deep breath and went in, half fearful of what she might find. There was, however, no sign of Lord Henry and no immediate sign of Jack, although they saw a small empty dish in a corner of the room. Lucy even checked the wardrobe, but there was no other indication that Jack had been there.

"I am going to the stables, Lucy. See if you can discover Lord Henry's whereabouts from any of the other servants, please."

"Yes, miss," said Lucy breathlessly, darting away on her mission.

A check of the stables brought no Jack, but it did bring news. One of the stableboys had seen Lord Henry taking a path toward the woods an hour or so ago. The boy had noticed him because he was out so early and because he was carrying a bag. "A game bag, it looked to be, Lady Hilary," he informed her. She hurried back to the house to change into her riding habit so that she could follow Lord Henry, fearful that he might finally have taken his vengeance upon them.

"Hilary!" said Lily stiffly, stopping on her way to the dining room for breakfast. "I assume that you and your friends are about to pack your bags and leave for Drake Hall."

"No, we are not," replied Hilary shortly. "Lord Henry has taken Jack, and I mean to find him before I go. I will certainly not leave Endicott without my dog."

"Nonsense!" said Lily sharply. "Henry has no interest in your dog. If Jack is gone, mark my words, he has run away. You must leave this morning, Hilary."

Before Hilary could respond, Lord Grayden, who had just stepped quietly from the library and overheard the last part of the conversation, spoke. "And why would Lady Hilary be leaving this morning, Lily?" he inquired pleasantly. "And why would you be instructing her that she must do so?"

Lily flushed. "That is between us, Grayden," she said hurriedly. "I assure you that this is in Hilary's best interests."

"Yes, I have noticed that you always put the interests of others ahead of your own," remarked Grayden dryly. "What is this about Jack?"

Lily hurried into speech once more before Hilary could reply. "Hilary has some wild notion that Henry must have taken Jack, simply because she cannot find him. Mark my words, the dog has run away to chase rabbits."

"I might be inclined to agree with Lily, Lord Grayden," Hilary said, moving past Lily so that she could go on to her room. "Except that Miss Brawley's abigail admitted that she gave Jack some drugged food last night while I was asleep, and that she then carried him to Lord Henry's chamber. One of the stableboys saw Lord Henry walking toward the woods this morning, carrying a bag. I am going to try to find him as soon as I change to my habit."

"And I will go with you," announced Grayden, turning back toward the library.

Lily was left to fume in the middle of the stairway,

angry that no one was concerned about her distress. She was still standing there a moment later when Grayden returned, adjusting the jacket that he had just put on once again.

"Oh, Grayden, if you only—" she began, but he cut her short.

"Lily, if I wish for any of my guests to depart, I shall tell them. You will not. Are we quite clear upon that point?" he asked, looking at her sternly.

"Well, if you only knew, Grayden, just what—"

"Lily, do you understand what I have said to you?" he interrupted.

"Yes, of course I do," she replied, pouting prettily. "But when Robert—"

"Robert would agree with my point completely," Grayden informed her, "and what's more, if he knew the high-handed manner in which you are treating Lady Hilary, I believe he would be particularly distressed."

Knowing that his point was entirely accurate, Lily turned on her heel and went back to her room, holding her head high and ignoring Hilary as she passed her on the stairs.

A few minutes of brisk cantering carried Hilary and Grayden through the copse that the stableboy had seen Lord Henry enter, and into the clearing beyond it. They had a clear view of several meadows, also dotted by small groves of trees, with a river winding lazily among them. In the distance, they could see several curls of smoke and a group of brightly painted wagons.

"Gypsies!" said Grayden, starting toward them. "They've come for the fair. It may be that they will have seen something of Henry or Jack. They usually know everything that is happening."

Wide-eyed, Hilary followed him into the encampment. She had always heard tales about Gypsies, but she had never actually been close to them. Her fingers fairly itched for her sketchbook as she looked at the striking collection of Romany faces before her. One in particular, an old woman with strong features and piercing dark eyes, was watching them from beside a campfire, studying them intently.

She remained mounted while Grayden swung down and strode toward a tall man who stepped forth from the others. She could not hear exactly what was being said, but she saw Grayden gesture toward her as he spoke, and the dark-skinned chieftain smiled at her appreciatively and executed a brief bow. Unfolding a sketch of Jack that Hilary had given him, he showed it to the Gypsy.

There was a perceptible pause as he studied it, then murmured something to the man standing next to him. Approaching Hilary, he held out the sketch and said, "So this is your little dog, my lady?"

She nodded. "Yes, Jack is mine. Have you seen him?" she asked eagerly.

He shrugged. "Perhaps, but then there are many small white dogs with a black marking just so. It is hard to tell."

"But you've seen one that looks something like this?" she persisted. "Did you see him this morning?"

"Perhaps, my lady, you should try to call him. Have you done so as you have been searching for him?"

Hilary looked at him for a moment, startled by his question. She had not, of course, since she had heard that Henry had drugged him.

"Do you mean that I should try calling him now?" she asked doubtfully, looking at all those gathered around to watch them.

He nodded. "What can you lose?" he asked. "If your dog hears you, he will come. If someone else's dog hears you, he may bark, but he will not come to you."

Hilary sat back a little in her saddle and cupped her

hand to her mouth. "Jack!" she called. "Jack, where are you, boy?"

For a moment there was stillness as they all listened. Finally, she heard a muffled barking.

"Jack! Come here, boy! Come on!" she called.

She saw the Gypsy chief motion toward one of the young men, who hurried out of sight. In a moment, Jack came running toward her, and Hilary swung down from the saddle and caught him up in her arms.

"Oh, thank you! Thank you!" she exclaimed, turning to the chief.

"It is our pleasure," he said, bowing. "We would not have accepted him if we had known he was your pet. We camp upon these lands each year for the fair, and we would not knowingly take something that belonged to the manor."

"How did you get him?" she asked, remembering Lord Henry walking in this direction.

"A gentleman from Endicott brought him here. He suggested that we enter him in the terrier races at Ilstead next month."

"Did he say that he was Jack's owner?" demanded Hilary.

The Gypsy nodded. "He said that the dog had gotten very difficult and sometimes bit children, so we should keep him locked in one of the carts most of the time."

"You would have done better to have locked the man in one of the carts," observed Hilary grimly. "He is far more dangerous than Jack."

The Gypsy laughed, a gold tooth flashing. "I think that the gentleman will wish that I had done so after you speak with him!"

"He will indeed," agreed Hilary, giving Jack to Lord Grayden to hold while she remounted her horse. Then she took him carefully in her arms. His run from the cart to her appeared to have taken most of his energy, and he rested gratefully against her with a minimum of wriggling.

"How do you wish for me to deal with Henry?" inquired Lord Grayden on their slow ride back to Endicott. "I realize that you would prefer that he be drawn and quartered, but since that is not one of my options, what is your next choice?"

Hilary shook her head. "I really don't know. He won't be sorry that he's done this; he'll just be sorry that he's been caught. So I don't know what would make him regret this."

"I think that I might have just the thing," remarked Grayden thoughtfully, gazing down at Jack.

"What will you do?" she asked curiously. "I hope that it is humiliating and exceedingly painful."

He nodded. "I will see what I can do, ma'am. Perhaps we can cause Henry at least a little embarrassment."

And Hilary had to be satisfied with that. They rode on for a few minutes in comfortable silence, enjoying the bright splendor of the morning.

"And so, Lady Hilary, did you plan to leave Endicott as Lily wished you to?" he asked finally, looking down at her.

"Yes, it seemed to me that would be the most reasonable thing to do. Clearly, I must return to the Brawleys, and they are creating misery for everyone here, so the sensible thing is to send them back to Drake Hall and for me to go with them."

"And tell me again why you must marry this man," he said.

She heaved a sigh of exasperation. "It is not because I wish to do so, Lord Grayden, but because I must. I need the income that he would provide for me."

"You have expensive tastes, I take it," he mused,

staring off into the distance as though meditating upon that point.

"Not particularly," she replied indignantly. "That is not the point of marrying him. I must have his income in order to keep a household and care for those who have placed their trust in me."

"Yes, Jack will assuredly need regular meals," he mused. "I can see that would take a considerable amount of money."

"It isn't just Jack," she demurred.

"So I understand," he agreed. "Whatever makes you feel that you must take of someone other than Jack and yourself?"

"Because others have taken care of me," she explained impatiently. "I need to return that favor when it is necessary, and I simply do not have the funds to do so. If I marry Mr. Brawley, I will have those funds."

"And that will be enough to make you happy?" he persisted.

"No, of course that will not be enough!" she replied tartly. "But it will have to do!"

"Well, I think that you are not requiring enough of the gentleman," he responded, shrugging his shoulders.

"And just what do you suggest that I ask of Mr. Brawley aside from his financial support?" she asked.

He stared into the distance for a moment as their horses kept moving steadily homeward.

"Graciousness," he said, "and an appreciation for you and your spirit."

She looked at him as though he had lost his mind. "I believe that those things will not be forthcoming," she informed him briskly.

And she tried not to think that those were things that she might be able to expect from a man such as Grayden—except, of course, that he already had a lover, and she knew that he was not the man she had imagined him to be.

They rode to the main entrance of the house, where one of the footmen took Jack from her and another helped her to dismount. Together with Jack, they entered the main hall, where Franklin bowed to Lord Grayden.

"Your guests are at breakfast, my lord," he said. "Would you like to go directly there, or would you like to change first?"

Lord Grayden turned to her. "Would you mind going in directly, Lady Hilary?" he asked. "With Jack, of course."

"Not at all," she responded. "I realize now that I have acquired quite an appetite this morning." She set Jack upon the floor, and he followed her quickly, moving a little more briskly than he had.

"Well!" said Lily, as they entered the room, glancing down at Jack. "I see that you found the dog after all. I told you that he had simply gone rabbiting."

"Yes," responded Grayden genially, turning his gaze to Lord Henry, whose eyes had grown a little larger, "Jack had chosen to go rabbiting among the Gypsies camped by the river."

"Gypsies!" exclaimed the Brawley sisters in chorus. "How wonderful!"

"They steal," announced their mother briefly, and Mr. Brawley nodded his head in solemn agreement.

"So I have heard," said Grayden, his eyes still on his cousin, "but they also purchase livestock of various sorts. Very sporting types, the Romanies. They enjoy a race of any sort."

"Yes, they come here because of the horse fair," agreed Lily. "You have told me that, Grayden."

"Yes, and occasionally someone is interested in dog

races," continued Grayden, "something like the terrier races over at Ilstead."

"Indeed?" responded Mrs. Brawley, sounded supremely disinterested. "I shouldn't think I would enjoy that at all."

"It appears," said Grayden, "that someone here felt that Jack might do well in the terrier races and presented him to the Gypsies to take with them when they leave."

The others, save for Lord Henry, stared at him.

"Did you give your dog to the Romanies?" asked Mrs. Brawley, looking at Hilary with disapproval. "I dislike the animal, of course, but I think that you should not have dealings with them. They cannot be trusted, you know."

"No, I don't believe I do know that," said Hilary crisply. "It seems to me that they are much more trustworthy than some under this very roof."

Lord Henry rose from his place at the table, but Grayden said pleasantly, "Do sit back down, Henry. We are not quite finished here."

"I have a business appointment," began Henry faintly, but Grayden cut him off.

"I am certain that you do, but you will not be keeping it. Instead, you will be taking a gift down to the Gypsy camp."

"Why would I do such a thing?" Lord Henry demanded. "I don't owe them anything!"

"I believe you do," said Grayden smoothly. "I think they will accept your gold snuffbox as an apology for presenting them with stolen goods. If they had been found with a stolen dog in their possession, it is likely that there would have been very unpleasant consequences for them—consequences that you would have brought upon them, Henry. So I believe that an apology on your part would be a good thing."

There was a lengthy pause while the others digested this. Henry had risen slowly, his face flushed with anger, but Grayden raised his hand to stop.

"You also owe an apology to Lady Hilary, Henry, and your word that this kind of thing will never happen again."

The apology was delivered in a low and angry voice, but it was delivered. Then the young man strode from the dining room.

"Well, I do say that this all seems very odd," complained Mrs. Brawley. "It does not seem to me that such things happen in well-run households. Why, at Drake Hall—"

"Yes, Mrs. Brawley, I am certain that at Drake Hall everything runs precisely as it should," interrupted Lily, weary of hearing from the Brawleys.

"Except, of course, that Miss Brawley's maid was a party to drugging Jack and removing him from my chamber last night," inserted Hilary grimly, determined to put that on the table. If she was going to have to return to Drake Hall, she would have no more trouble about Jack.

Ophelia gasped, and even Mrs. Brawley looked startled.

"Well, how very tiresome this all is!" complained Lily. "Grayden, are we to be bored to tears by all of this? What of the Gypsies and the fair? Shall we be going?"

For once, Lily appeared to have struck a chord, for everyone—with the exception of Mr. Brawley—felt that her question was a good one.

"Ah, yes, Grayden! Yes, indeed we must go!" Lily announced. "It is only right that you provide some amusement for your guests, and what better than a fair to do so?"

Ophelia and Deidre were clearly in favor of such an

outing, as long as Lord Grayden planned to escort them, and their mother appeared to agree, despite her disapproval of the Gypsies.

"Who knows what we will see?" remarked Ophelia. "Why, there might even be a Gypsy fortune teller!"

Deidre giggled at the idea of going to a fortune teller, but Hilary was charmed. A fair! And the Gypsies again! She would have sketches of Gypsies and their horses and their crystal balls. She became almost as impatient as Lily in her desire to attend the fair, so it was fortunate that it was to begin the very next day.

The ladies watched the skies all during the remainder of the day, fearful of rain, but the sunshine remained steady, and they made their preparations with excitement. Jack appeared to have recovered nicely, and Hilary had been spared any further sight of Lord Henry, who had gone into seclusion in his chamber.

Hilary and Lucy tucked Jack firmly into his basket that night, and Lucy offered to sleep on a pallet before the door to prevent any further dognappings. Hilary was not troubled by any fear of Henry, however, for she was certain that he would not openly defy Lord Grayden. For the time, at least, Jack was safe.

She applied herself diligently to her sketches that evening, attempting to catch the faces of the Gypsy leader and of the old woman by the fire. Her favorite for the evening, however, was of Jack sprinting toward her, his tail held high.

Nineteen

Endicott was a whirl of activity the next morning, for everyone was preparing to go to the fair. Mrs. Brawley slowed progress upon several occasions by offering her suggestions for protecting themselves from the thieving Romanies, but Ophelia finally led her to one side and promised that Raymond would remain at her side during the entire outing. Fortunately for the rest of them, that seemed to comfort the lady. Naturally, Hilary thought the arrangement a brilliant one, for she would be relieved of Mr. Brawley's constant presence for the entire day. He would be fully occupied by his mother, whose fears were many. She did not even have to contend with his company in the carriage, for he and Lord Grayden rode alongside the ladies. Lord Henry had chosen to remain at home.

When they arrived at the fairgrounds, a broad swath of golden meadows outside the village, Hilary's attention was attracted first by the Gypsy chieftain, who was bargaining with a farmer over a handsome bay. By the time they had found a place for the carriage, however, and joined the crowd of merrymakers, she could not immediately find him. Disappointed, she promised herself that she would be able to draw his face from memory.

"My lady!" Hilary glanced up sharply, for her attention had been caught by a group of children at a nearby Punch-and-Judy show. "Did you and your little dog make it safely home yesterday?" the Gypsy chief inquired, bowing to her with a smile.

"Yes, yes, we did," she assured him, returning the smile. "And I thank you again for returning him to me."

His eyes shone with amusement. "As I told you yesterday, my lady, it was our pleasure. Indeed, I did not fully realize how great a pleasure it had been until yesterday afternoon."

Here he reached into the pocket of his jacket and withdrew a snuffbox of gleaming gold, daintily engraved with scrollwork. "I had no idea that we would receive a reward," he remarked. "Perhaps you need another dog."

Hilary laughed and shook her head. "No, Jack will do, thank you. And I am certain that Lord Henry was glad to reward you," she added.

The Romany nodded, schooling his countenance into a grave expression. "Indeed, yes. I could see that he would have liked to have given me even more."

He paused a moment, then said, "Your little dog . . . Is he at the manor today?"

Hilary nodded. "Why do you ask?"

"And the man you called Lord Henry, is he here with you today?"

"No, he chose to remain at Endicott," she replied slowly.

"Perhaps there is someone there who is looking after your pet," he suggested, noting her troubled expression.

"Yes, my maid will take care of him," she replied, thinking to herself that Lucy might need to be taken care of herself if Lord Henry decided to misbehave. Surely, Lord Henry would not be such a fool as to bring more trouble down upon himself.

"All is well then," smiled the Gypsy, nodding in approval. "Then you may enjoy yourself today without worrying about your dog."

"Yes, I intend to enjoy myself," she responded automatically, trying to put all thought of trouble out of her mind. Certainly, she told herself, after the punishment that Grayden had dealt his cousin, he would not dare to create a problem either for Lucy or for Jack.

Nonetheless, it was fully an hour before she could finally put the thought from her mind. Undoubtedly all was well and she was once again making a mountain from a molehill, as she was often inclined to do.

She had wandered over to watch some of the bargaining taking place for the horses. A shaggy Shetland pony was sold to a young boy who looked as small and sturdy and shaggy as the pony itself. Smiling with pleasure, she tucked away the mental sketch of the pair for later. A yeoman farmer in gaiters and a bright jacket argued violently with a small man who bore a striking resemblance to a weasel, and they both turned to glare at the farmer who was herding a small flock of sheep through the part of the meadow occupied by the horse traders.

"What do you think?" asked Lord Grayden softly, coming up quietly behind her and leaning over her shoulder to whisper into her ear. "Have you found a horse for yourself?"

Hilary laughed and moved away. "I shall ride your horses while I am at Endicott, and when I go to Drake Hall, I shall ride Mr. Brawley's," she replied. "I am not in the market for a new horse."

"Very wise," he murmured. "Most of these men, especially the Gypsies, drive a very shrewd bargain. I don't doubt that you would be left in the dust."

Hilary bristled. "I assure you that I could bargain with these men, Lord Grayden, and do so successfully.

I simply do not have the money to make such a purchase at the moment."

"That is just as well," he replied, still looking patronizing.

Irritated, Hilary turned and walked away from him, leaving him to stare after her. He was a most annoying man, she decided. She undoubtedly provided him with amusement when she allowed him to see that he was bothering her. Once again she resolved that she would not allow his behavior to bother her.

"My lady!" called the Gypsy chieftain, waving at her in the distance. "Come and see the colt!"

Doing as she had been bid, Hilary arrived at his side in time to see a handsome little foal being loaded onto a cart. Standing close beside the cart were Tom and Priscilla Tiller. Priscilla saw her and waved her over.

"Is he yours?" Hilary asked, gesturing to the foal.

Priscilla nodded with pride. "Squire Gaines just bought him from Tom. His sire won a good many races here, and Tom thinks he'll be just such another one."

"I'm surprised you're selling him then," Hilary observed. "If he is going to be fast, Tom could race him, couldn't he?"

Priscilla shook her head. "It takes a great deal of money to keep a racehorse, my lady. That is not for the likes of us. And then, too, we shall soon have another child to care for."

Her cheeks glowed at the announcement, and Hilary congratulated her sincerely. "You are a fortunate woman," she observed. "And your child is fortunate to be born into such a family."

"Thank you, my lady," replied Priscilla. She paused a moment, studying Hilary's face. "Do you still have the rosemary?" she asked in a low voice, glancing toward her husband, who was busily talking to another horse dealer.

Hilary nodded. "I shall do as you said and put it under my pillow tonight," she assured Priscilla.

"I did it myself," Priscilla informed her proudly. "My mother gave me a sprig of rosemary and told me it was for remembrance. Then she said that if I put it under my pillow on All Hallow's and dreamed about a man, it would be the man I would marry."

She paused and smiled. "I dreamed about Tom, and he asked me if we could have the banns published in church the next Sunday."

"Why rosemary?" asked Hilary curiously.

Priscilla shook her head. "I don't know. Rosemary is for remembrance, and my mother always said that a dream is like remembering something before it happens," she replied.

"Good afternoon, Priscilla, Lady Hilary," said Lord Grayden cheerfully, descending upon them suddenly. "May I persuade the two of you to join me at the gingerbread booth for some refreshments?"

Priscilla smiled and shook her head. "That's very kind of you, my lord," she replied, "but Tom is almost finished with his business and we'll be starting for home before too very long."

"You're not staying for the dancing and the bonfire tonight?" asked Grayden, and she shook her head again.

"I need my rest, sir, and Tom has to be out in the field early tomorrow morning."

"Have a safe journey home," he responded, bowing to her and leading Hilary toward the gingerbread booth.

"Remember what I said, Lady Hilary," called Priscilla after them. "Rosemary is for remembrance."

Grayden looked down at Hilary, his brow faintly creased. "That's a very cryptic farewell," he observed. "What does it mean?"

"Merely, I believe, sir, that rosemary is indeed a symbol of remembrance."

Grayden eyed her speculatively, but he said no more, instead plying her with gingerbread and apple cider. Since he was behaving in a more mannerly fashion, Hilary enjoyed herself hugely until they were joined by Lily, who still seemed strongly inclined to enumerate the ways in which the others had abused her.

"Undoubtedly you will soon be canonized and we shall all know you as Saint Lily," said Grayden finally, having had more than he could bear of her complaints.

"Well, you needn't be so insulting about it, Grayden!" Lily snapped. "You have no idea what aggravation I am having to put up with. You two have just gone your own way and abandoned me to the Brawleys!"

"I would feel sorrier for you, Lily, were I not about to be abandoned to the Brawleys myself," responded Hilary. "And I shall be abandoned to them for a much longer time."

Grayden looked down at Lily and shook his head in agreement. "I must say, Lily, that you shouldn't begrudge Hilary a few minutes on her own. All too soon what she says will be true. You, on the other hand, need only be aggravated by them for a few more minutes."

In the distance, they heard a familiar voice calling Grayden's name, and Ophelia's thin red scarf being waved in the air.

"Hurry!" Lord Grayden urged Hilary. "If we are fortunate, we will escape."

"Don't leave me!" protested Lily. "I don't want to be—"

"Just think of yourself as a sacrificial offering, Lily," Lord Grayden called as they disappeared into the crowd. "Now you have a reason to suffer! You won't have to pretend! Think of your canonization!"

Laughing, the two of them ran, abandoning Lily to her fate.

"It does seem too bad," observed Hilary when she could catch her breath. "After all, Lily is badly outnumbered by the Brawleys."

Lord Grayden shook his head. "Lily is equal to any number of Brawleys," he said firmly. "I have no doubt that she will emerge unscathed from any encounter with them."

Once again Hilary thought how very unloverlike some of his comments about Lily were. Still, she had seen them together, and she knew what Lily had to say about him. Lord Grayden was most certainly her favored escort. For a moment she thought about Lord Carhill but decided that doing so would cast a pall upon the day.

"What were you thinking just then?" asked Grayden curiously.

"Why do you ask?" she countered, angry with herself. He seemed to be able to read her expressions with exasperating ease.

"I saw that shadow pass over your face," he replied, watching her closely. "It was just like watching a cloud pass over the sun."

When she didn't answer, he continued, "Of course, I suppose that you are more like the moon than the sun. After all, your hair is silver, not golden."

He put out his hand and fingered a loose curl gently, and she drew away.

"Do you find me so very distasteful, Lady Hilary?" he asked gently. "You pull away from me whenever I come close to you. I am not a vain man, but I know that is not the way most women react to me."

"Ah no, not vain at all," she returned lightly. "You are, in effect, telling me that other women find you attractive and wondering why I do not."

Grayden nodded. "Yes, I suppose that's exactly what I'm telling you," he said.

"Lily finds you most appealing," she said, looking off into the distance instead of returning his gaze.

"Lily finds many men appealing," he responded. "That is no test."

"How very unchivalrous you are toward her," replied Hilary slowly, turning to look at him. "Why are you not kinder to someone who loves you?"

"Who loves me?" he repeated incredulously. "Are you speaking of Lily, Lady Hilary?"

"Of course I'm speaking of Lily!" she returned impatiently. "Who else would I be speaking of?"

"Almost anyone," he replied. "Have you not noticed, Lady Hilary, that Lily loves no one but herself?"

"But you—" Hilary began. "I know that you love Lily."

"Is that what you've been thinking?" he demanded, laughing and pulling her close to him, ignoring the passing crowd as they stood in the shadows of an old oak. An early twilight was falling, and the air was growing sharp.

"Why would I not think that?" she asked. "What else was I to think when the two of you travel together to rescue me from Drake Hall, and when I see the two of you forever in each other's pocket? What could I think?"

He leaned down to kiss her, but Hilary fled. Hearing him dismiss Lily with such ease unnerved her, for she had thought that he was at least true to his lover. Now she had to readjust her thinking completely. Lily was not, and never had been, according to him, his lover. What was she to think?

The dark was gathering rapidly around her and she knew that Grayden was close behind her. Seeing the flap of a tent open briefly, revealing the glow of candlelight within, Hilary headed for it and ducked inside.

Beside a small table sat the old Gypsy woman she had seen at the camp yesterday morning. Hilary recognized her immediately; then her eyes fell upon the glowing crystal ball on the table.

"Come here, my lady," crooned the old woman, patting the stool next to her. "I will look into your future and tell you all that you need to know to prepare for it."

Fascinated, Hilary seated herself and looked deep into the crystal ball, in which she could see the reflected glow of the candlelight but little else.

"I see a man," murmured the old woman, wrapping her scarlet shawl more closely about her shoulders. "A man who has made many sacrifices for others."

Hilary looked up from the crystal ball. The Gypsy was undoubtedly conjuring this up out of whole cloth. Certainly neither her father nor Mr. Brawley had ever made a sacrifice for anyone.

"Who is it?" she asked. "What does he look like?"

The Gypsy looked into the ball again. "Tall," she responded. "He is very tall, taller than you, my lady. And he loves you."

"You know who she is talking about, don't you, Lady Hilary?" inquired Lord Grayden gently, having let himself into the tent to listen to what was being said.

"I know you are tall," replied Hilary in a faint voice, staring into his neckcloth and avoiding his eye. "You're the only man I must look up to."

"And that is precisely as it should be," he responded lightly, tilting her chin toward his face. "And what do you see when you look up at me? Do you see the eyes of a man in love?"

What she saw was once again the treacherous tenderness in his eyes. He was, she thought, far too well schooled in flirtation. Despite her best intentions, she leaned toward him and their lips met. Hilary pulled sharply away and started toward the entrance of the tent.

"Where are you going?" he demanded. "Why won't you let me kiss you?"

Remembering Lily and all the hours he had spent dancing attendance upon her, she knew that she was unconvinced that there was nothing between them.

"Lord Carhill," she said firmly, without looking at him. And she raised the tent flap and stepped out into the night.

"Carhill?" he asked, following her into the darkness. "What does he have to do with whether or not you allow me to kiss you?"

"More than you can imagine," she replied, doing her best to move away from him. Say what he might, she could not imagine that he and Lily had not once been in love, even if that were no longer true. And in that case, he had still betrayed Lord Carhill and showed himself a man unworthy of her trust.

"I am planning to stay with you, Lady Hilary, so you might as well make up your mind to it," he said grimly, not allowing her to escape. "And Carhill is a worthy man, but he has a wife whom he loves."

In the distance, they could see the flickering lights of candles, set in hollowed gourds that rimmed the wooden dance platform, erected especially for the occasion. As they neared it, Hilary could see that the gourds had been carved in a wild variety of designs: faces, flowers, lacework patterns. Their eerie glow lit the darkness, and on a hill beyond them, a huge bonfire blazed to keep away the spirits abroad on All Hallow's Eve.

The music enfolded them, and Grayden whispered, "Come now, ma'am, even if you do despise me, how can you not dance on such a night as this? Dance with me tonight, and hate me tomorrow with all your heart."

Hilary looked at the laughing couples on the platform and made her decision. Tomorrow she would be leaving Endicott with the Brawleys. Tonight she deserved to dance!

"Very well, Lord Grayden," she replied coolly, holding out her hand to him. "Tonight we shall dance."

And dance they did. Not until the players put away their instruments did they stop. Miss Brawley had attempted to intervene and seize Lord Grayden as her partner, as had Lily, but he would not allow it. He and Hilary danced, and he allowed no one else to intervene. Mr. Brawley watched them for only a short space because his mother noticed that two of the musicians were Gypsies, and she did not wish to remain so dangerously close to them.

By the time the carriage had disgorged them at the front door of Endicott, all of them asked nothing more than a good night's rest. Not even Ophelia had anything to say before retiring for the evening.

When Hilary got to her chamber, the sight of Jack asleep in his basket comforted her, and she climbed wearily into bed. Before she drifted off to sleep, however, she remembered the rosemary and tucked it carefully under her pillow. Perhaps by tomorrow morning she would have seen the face of the man she was to marry.

She was well into her dream, walking lazily across a meadow in a gown of cornflower blue, when she saw a man walking toward her. Increasing her pace, she hurried toward him, eager to see his face.

Faintly she heard Jack growl, but she ignored it. When she heard the door of her room click open, however, and saw someone entering, candle in hand, she sat straight up in bed.

"Who's there?" she demanded, frightened by the unexpected intrusion. When Jack's growl faded, however, she relaxed, knowing that it must be a friend.

Peering into the light, she saw Lord Grayden's face, looking oddly unfamiliar in the flickering light of the candle.

"What is it, Lord Grayden?" she demanded. "Has something happened?"

He nodded. "I did not think you would wish to wait until morning to know," he replied.

"To know what?" she asked, growing fearful. "Is there something amiss?"

"Not unless you have taken me in dislike, my dear," returned Miss Dunsmore cheerfully, stepping from behind Lord Grayden.

"Clara!" she shrieked, bouncing to her feet. "Clara! What are you doing here? Did my father force you to leave?"

Miss Dunsmore shook her head. "Why, no, Hilary. You sent for me, my dear. Don't you remember?"

"I sent for you?" Hilary said blankly. "I am delighted that you are here, Clara," she added hurriedly, not wishing to seem inhospitable, "but I'm not quite sure how it happened."

"Lord Grayden has been kindness itself," said Miss Dunsmore, her voice breaking. "Why, I had a carriage all to myself, and a hot brick for my feet, and outriders—just as though I were a lady of consequence."

"And so you are," replied Lord Grayden. Seeing Hilary still staring at him, he added, "You left your letter in the library the other night, and I'm afraid that I read it to see what had upset you so. And of course I could not leave things as they were after reading about Miss Dunsmore's problem."

"No, of course not," said Hilary, bemused by his

explanation. "Clara, come and sit by me," she said, regaining a little of her composure and patting the bed.

"No, my dear, you go back to sleep. My room is being prepared, but dear Lord Grayden wanted to surprise you tonight instead of tomorrow morning. Are you pleased?" she asked hopefully.

"Pleased?" Hilary repeated. "I am delighted." And she tried not to think of what it would be like the next morning when they began to pack for their move. Poor Clara would have scarcely any time here.

Miss Dunsmore said good night and went with a maid to be shown to her chamber, leaving Grayden still watching Hilary.

"Well, tell me, ma'am," he said, "did the rosemary work? Did you dream of me tonight?"

Hilary was grateful for the comparative darkness, for she felt her cheeks turning scarlet. "Why would I have dreamed of you, sir?" she demanded. "And what rosemary are you talking about?"

"The rosemary that I asked Priscilla Tiller to give to you," he said, setting the candle on a chest and walking closer to her.

"You asked her to give it to me?" she gasped. "Why?"

"Because I wanted to have some way to force you to think of me, my dear, and I hoped that this might do it. Priscilla had told me about her mother giving the rosemary to her—and that Tom had proposed the very next day."

He grinned at her. "And I firmly believe that her mother and Tom worked that out between them. Priscilla was the prettiest girl in the village, so she could have had her pick of young men."

"But they couldn't have arranged to have Priscilla dream of him," Hilary pointed out practically.

"Oh, I'm not entirely certain," he demurred. "Her

mother wanted her to marry him, and she told Priscilla stories about him just before she went to sleep, trying to plant the thought in her mind. At any rate, it worked."

Hilary sat still, staring at him. "But why did you want me to have the rosemary?" she asked blankly.

"Why, so that you might dream of me, of course. And speaking of that," he added, "have you dreamed yet of a man?"

She nodded.

"Who was it?" he inquired a little anxiously.

Hilary shook her head. "I haven't the least notion," she replied. "You awoke me before I could see his face."

Lord Grayden looked a little disappointed for a moment, but then he smiled once more. "Well, just in case you hadn't dreamed of me, I thought that I would be certain that you saw me again tonight. Fortunately, Miss Dunsmore arrived at an opportune moment."

"Your timing was excellent," she said thoughtfully.

He bowed. "I appreciate whatever kind words I receive, ma'am," he replied. "And now I will leave you to finish your night's rest."

As he picked up the candlestick and turned, he glanced at the stack of sketches she had been looking through and froze. Leaving her bed to see what had so attracted him, she saw that he was looking at the sketch of Lily and Lord Carhill in which she was perched on the arm of his chair, looking at him with an expression of deep affection.

"Do you like it?" she asked a little anxiously, for he continued to stare at it as though transfixed. "I know that it needs work. It's only a rough sketch."

"I love it," he said, his voice deep with emotion. "Tell me why you drew this, Hilary."

"Because that is the way I wish things were for Lord

Carhill and Lily," she said hesitantly. "I call them my 'what-if' sketches. I draw them and then hope that seeing them and thinking about them will help to make them come true."

"My uncle would like to have this," he said slowly, still looking at it. "Perhaps you can give it to him when he arrives tomorrow."

Hilary's expression brightened. "Lord Carhill is coming?" she exclaimed. "I am so glad to hear it!"

Grayden nodded. "He is feeling better and is coming to take full charge of Lily again," he said. "I am anxious to relinquish my responsibility to him."

"What do you mean?" she asked, staring at him. "What responsibility?"

"Lily," he replied. "When my uncle became so ill in Italy, he wrote to me and asked me to watch over Lily until he was well enough to do so again. She was too wild and young to be left unchaperoned and he was afraid for her."

"You were her *chaperone?*" Hilary demanded. "Not her lover?"

"Most definitely not her lover," he assured her. "In fact, if I did not love my uncle, I would have deserted my post long ago."

"But you did not," she said fondly, running her hand lightly over his cheek.

"No, I did not," he agreed. "But that, dear lady, is enough about my uncle and more than enough about Lily. Now I wish to tell your fortune."

He lowered his voice mysteriously. "You see before you a tall man, a very tall man." He pulled her close to him and folded her against his waistcoat, whispering into her hair, "A man who loves you. I promise you, my lady, that I will try to make you a very happy woman."

Jack, who had gone back to his basket, growled throatily as he chased his imaginary rabbits.

"I believe, sir, that you have a little Gypsy blood," said Hilary, drawing his face down to hers. "I shall have to watch you carefully."

The kiss was long and tender and scented with the fragrance of rosemary. As she emerged briefly from his embrace, Hilary looked up at him, puzzled. "I must still be smelling the rosemary from under my pillow," she said.

Grayden laughed, opening his waistcoat and pulling another bunch of rosemary, also bound with a scarlet ribbon, from an inner pocket. "Priscilla gave this to me today. She likes you very well, you know, and she thought that I should have some rosemary of my own, so that I could dream of you."

"And what if you dream of someone else, dear sir?" she inquired, smiling up at him. "Or what if I had do?"

"I could dream of no one else," he replied, pressing her close again. "And I have every intention of forcing you to dream about me, even if I must come in here and whisper my name until it drifts into your dreams."

"You realize, sir," she said softly, taking the rosemary and crushing it gently between her fingers so that its piquancy filled the room, "that there was no need for the rosemary. My dreams were already filled with you."

As he folded her once more in his arms, she whispered, "Our first daughter will be named Rosemary. . . ."

Silence fell upon the chamber and Jack slept on, as a sprig of crushed rosemary drifted down and draped across his muzzle.

Epilogue

"Rosemary! Where are you?" called Hilary. "Robert? Clara? Jack?"

As she stood on the terrace, waiting for any sign of life from her family, the haunting fragrance of burning leaves reminded her that autumn was upon them once again. She had seen the Gypsy caravan roll past Endicott yesterday morning, once more leaving the valley after the fair.

A sharp bark in the distance told her that Jack, at least, had heard her. A moment later, Miss Dunsmore emerged from the puzzle maze, her glasses askew and her hair disordered.

"We are coming, Hilary dear," she said reassuringly. "But just at the moment I can't find the children. Don't worry, though, I'll have them in just a moment."

Before she could plunge back into the maze, Rosemary, her silver hair floating behind her, raced through the green arch, her brother Robert tumbling out just behind her.

"Well, Jack? Are you lost?" Hilary called. "Everyone else is here. Are you coming?"

In response, Jack came burrowing under the hedge, his shiny black nose and white muzzle appearing first. After a minute or two of concentrated wriggling, he managed to extricate himself completely and shot across the lawn, running a set of figure eights to show his delight at a safe return to civilization.

"Come along in," said Hilary. "Aunt Lily and Uncle Robert have arrived, and they're waiting for us."

"Hurrah!" shouted Robert. "Byron and Hilary are here!"

Hilary smiled to herself as the children rushed inside to see their cousins. Lily had at first found it a little difficult to share Lord Carhill's attention with their children, but—with age and the help of her husband—she had become kinder and more generous. Unquestionably, though, Hilary's children loved their uncle. He had long since recovered his health, and his third marriage had proved to be the blessing of his later years.

Before she went in to join her husband and children and their guests, she paused a moment beside a pot of herbs that sat in the late October sun. Smiling, she picked a sprig of rosemary and crushed it between her fingers.

No need to retreat into dreams or a what-if world of sketches any longer, she mused. Much to her father's delight and the Brawleys' chagrin, she and Lord Grayden had married that very first autumn. Her sketchbooks now were filled with her family and her garden and Jack—and an occasional Gypsy.

"Are you coming, Hilary?" asked her husband, standing at the door and holding out his hand to her.

Together they strolled into the drawing room, the fragrance of rosemary drifting in behind them.

ABOUT THE AUTHOR

Mona Gedney lives with her family in Indiana and is the author of eleven Zebra Regency romances. Mona loves to hear from readers, and you may write to her c/o Zebra Books. Please include a self-addressed, stamped envelope if you wish a response.

More Zebra Regency Romances

Discover the Romances of
Hannah Howell

Discover The Magic of
Romance With
Jo Goodman

Embrace the Romances of
Shannon Drake

BOOK YOUR PLACE ON OUR WEBSITE AND MAKE THE READING CONNECTION!

We've created a customized website just for our very special readers, where you can get the inside scoop on everything that's going on with Zebra, Pinnacle and Kensington books.

When you come online, you'll have the exciting opportunity to:

- View covers of upcoming books
- Read sample chapters
- Learn about our future publishing schedule (listed by publication month *and author*)
- Find out when your favorite authors will be visiting a city near you
- Search for and order backlist books from our online catalog
- Check out author bios and background information
- Send e-mail to your favorite authors
- Meet the Kensington staff online
- Join us in weekly chats with authors, readers and other guests
- Get writing guidelines
- AND MUCH MORE!

**Visit our website at
http://www.zebrabooks.com**